M000073295

MASSÉ

Written by:
Tim DuBetz

Special thank you...

Molly DuBetz
T.J. DuBetz
Cheryl Naanes
Jim Burnett
Jamie Rouleau
Rocky Hank Milner
Anita Clegg Cravens
Timothy Lemasters Dupree
Anthony Nichols/Meliah Rage

My family, friends, followers, fans, YOU, and anyone else who enjoys my writings, I sincerely appreciate your continued support and inspiration.

<u>Introduction</u>:

Joe Williams. Named after his Father, he's a young black man with a good heart but a street attitude except when it comes to his "Pops". Twenty two years old, agnostic, born and raised in south-side Chicago, lost his mother, Shelia, when he was 6. His mother was considered the "Princess Diana" of Chicago by her closest friends. She was a lighter skinned very attractive woman who never had a bad word to say about anyone. She was an innocent bystander in a local liquor store robbery gone wrong, she was just in there to cash a check and pick up some milk. The gunman was kind of taken in by her figure and wanted to "see that ass". He put his gun hand in between her shoulder blades to forcefully bend her over a bit, the barrel of the gun at the base of her neck. As he was pushing her over he accidentally squeezed the trigger. Sheila was working the snack counter in a local theater and rumors were she also worked some customers in a backroom for extra money while the movies were playing…you know what they say about rumors though. Sheila's flirty attitude and jealous women probably fueled the rumors more than anything else. In a shit society where people hear you but don't listen, until it's too late, Sheila was different, she went out of her way to make things happen. She didn't poke her nose into other people's business, didn't waste her time spreading political hate and if she asked you what was wrong it's because she genuinely cared. She was the kind of person that just wanted to make other people happy, that's what made her happy. Whether it was Joe's request or a neighbors, Sheila had everyone's back and she didn't make excuses, as long as it didn't interfere with home. Joe and little Joe's needs and wants came first. That happiness reaction she received from others was her drug. This is where Joe gets his heart from.

Joe was raised by his Father who never attended school. Sr's own mother lived boyfriend to boyfriend, and they could change daily. No one could satisfy her, she had to be the center of attention 24/7. Most people just considered her a bitch, she offered nothing but expected everything, she wasn't even moderately attractive. She made a living on her knees to hook a guy as soon as she lost one. She had blown so many men that some were repeats and she had no idea who they were. She didn't know who Joe's father was nor did she care. Sr's own education was through television programming.

Losing Sheila really took a lot out of Joe Sr. He said once that when he met her he found purpose in life, that the simplicity she offered made sense to him. He lived for her because she lived for him. Joe lived with the "backroom" rumors and never asked her about them. He had convinced himself if they were true, she was only doing what was financially best for the family, just business nothing personal. Sheila's murder created a great hatred for the world in Joe's heart that remains even today, he pushes on only because of the son he had with her. After a couple years of mourning Joe made an effort to replace Sheila, he was never successful…the world is laden with typical rather than unique and once you've had unique…typical just doesn't cut it. Having given up on his unicorn search Joe tends to entertain younger girls when he's feeling lonely, they're more energetic and carry less baggage. Joe had fancied himself a pool player but supported himself and his son as a handyman doing odd jobs around the city and working part time as a fast food employee. Joe Sr. had been playing pool his whole life but never reached that upper echelon, still he was better than the average player. Though he pretty much just plays for recreation now, Joe did spend some time as a gambler of the game in his younger years. He faced many professional hustlers like "Pretty Boy Floyd", "The Sandman", "St. Louie" Louie, "Bucky Bell", "Cornbread Red", and even "The Priest". Joe never beat these guys but he loved playing them because they were characters. The Priest had the biggest impact on him. They had played a few sets and The Priest broke Joe and his backer. Six thousand dollars in the hole and with nothing left Joe offered his stick and a night with his then girlfriend as a wager against one thousand dollars, "it's all I got left" he said "and she said it was ok.". The Priest thought about it for a second then shook his head. "You know Joe, a lot of people gamble at pool for the rush, tension, ego or even hope that it makes their opponent play worse or themselves better. This is just a job to me, I don't even think about the money, I just make balls, that's my job. She looks like she'd be fun but when I lay with a woman it has to be her desire to do so, not because she's getting paid, forced or out of obligation, these things tend to take the genuine fun and sincerity out of it. Also, never bet "all you got" because when you lose it, and you will, you've got nothing. Know when you're beat Joe, know when you can't win and just walk away, there's no shame in that. You should have walked away four sets ago. Playing pool isn't a scratch off ticket. Sure there's some luck in it but the better player will win ninety nine percent of the time, it doesn't matter what's on the line, nothing or a million dollars, the better player will win more than not…know when you're not the better player Joe." After he spoke he sighed then reached in his pocket and laid five hundred dollars on the table, he looked at Joe and said "A smart person could double that in a couple of days, a dumb one could lose it in an hour, which one are you Joe?" then turned, donned his trench coat, tipped his head to Joe's girlfriend "Miss" he said and walked out.

Pops always took little Joe with him to the pool hall. When little Joe was twelve the owner of the local pool hall gave him an older Brunswick cue stick that someone had left behind but never returned to claim. It was beat up a bit but it rolled straight and had a good tip on it. While "Pops" was playing five or ten dollar games little Joe would be banging balls on the table in the corner trying to emulate shots he watched other players make. Occasionally a player would stop on the way to the counter or bathroom and offer him a quick tip or lesson. Joe Jr. dropped out of high school at 16, not because he wasn't smart enough but because he has a problem with authority, he also believes he can make a living at playing pool and that school is standing in the way of practice. About four years ago when Joe turned 18 he joined a local league and quickly became one of their better players. Everybody in Chicago knew little Joe could play some pool but no one considered him among the elite of the city. Joe would play for a buck or two here and there but he wasn't a high dollar player so no one took him too seriously. Sadly, the more you're willing to bet, the higher your stature in the pool world. Joe had some flaws in his game, and in his mind, but he has some dreams of playing in the big shows. Joe was kind of taking after his Dad and doing odd jobs for money so he never had a lot of it for gambling, just enough for league and the occasional date night with his girlfriend "Tish". Joe lives at a crossroads in life, he has his mother's heart but his fathers world resentment. It's a tough way to go through life when you can see everything as both beautiful and ugly, both fearful and pleasurable. Like being scared to make a decision so you don't make one, you just conform to "whatever" comes your way…and that will slowly deteriorate you on the inside where identity becomes nothing but a black hole, and like a black hole it can effect everyone around you.

In recent months Pops had been noticing some changes to his sons demeanor, much less talkative, head always down, almost depressive, this is about where our story begins…

<u>Regrets</u>:

With his cue stick in its case, and over his shoulder, Joe's walking home from the pool hall having just lost his 9 ball league match. His head hanging low, he's not feeling like much of a pool player. Joe's considered one of the best in his league, and he feels he should beat everyone regardless of the handicap size and when he doesn't he feels like he lets the team down. He also believes people think less of him as a player. It's sometimes tough on a player's mind to lose to someone who's getting a huge spot but who you could crush playing even, but such is amateur pool.

Joe walks into his apartment building, makes his way up the four flights of stairs to he and his pops apartment. He opens the door and closes it, turns to find a completely naked young woman on the couch laying on her stomach watching television. Without offering any indication of shame she turns and says "Hi.", Joe offers no acknowledgment other than an upward tilt of his head but takes a second look at her ass as he heads towards the kitchen.

Entering the kitchen pops is to the right in nothing but his boxers waiting for the coffee to finish brewing.

Joe: "How old is this one pops?"
Pops: "Hey Joe, she's 18, been seeing her a couple weeks, why?"
Joe: "Yeah right, 18 year old mouth with a 15 year old ass,

these girls gonna get you in trouble pops."

Pops: "She's fine ain't she? I like this one, she's a bit of a freak, makes me feel alive."

Joe: "You ain't gonna feel alive in the joint pops, you're gonna hate life more than you do now. Or maybe you don't make the joint because some pissed off Dad or boyfriend decides to take it out on you themselves."

Pops: "Joe come on, we're just having fun, we ain't hurting nobody."

Just as Joe was about to say something else a hand with a drivers license was put in his face from behind with a girls voice shouting "I'm 18 and I fuck who I want, when I want, where I want and I don't need your permission, his, or anyone else's." Joe turns to see the girl from the couch directly behind him, still nude, as she continues. "Sounds like you just pissed off 'cuz you ain't hitting this." Joe just shakes his head and walks out to the living room.

Pops.: "Why don't you give us an hour. Go home, refresh, maybe put on some lingerie, come back about 11, let me talk to Joe."

Girl: "OK baby, I'll be back at 11." She exits to the bedroom and emerges dressed, as she heads towards the door she looks at little Joe and says "I'm a screamer, I'll be back at 11, if you don't want to hear it, don't be here." She leaves.

Walking out of the kitchen pops says "What the fuck Joe? Is

2

my sex life the reason why you're so pissed off and depressed lately?"

Joe sighs: "Yeah, kind of Pops. You look like you're over here having a good time and enjoying life and I'm over here hating it and I know you still miss Mom."

Pops: "Yeah Joe I do, more than you or anyone else will ever know but it's been 16 years, the fact is I'm still alive and have to go on, I still got bills to pay, I still wanna feel good, ain't gonna do me no good to live out my life as a hermit. I ain't no drinker, I don't do drugs, I don't beat you, I ain't no thief and I ain't breaking no laws Joe. It ain't about love and it ain't about replacing your mom, it's just about having fun, nothing else."

Joe: "Yeah Dad but some of these girls…I mean damn, they young."

Pops: "Joe, is this really what's eating at you? I mean you been this way for a few months, you ain't said shit about them before. You said you were hating life, why don't you tell me why."

Joe: "I'm sorry pops, it ain't the girls, I'm just tired of my life. I'm tired of losing to players who got no business being on the same table as me, tired of spotting players three racks who can run out just as easily as me, tired of playing around a bunch of loud drunks who don't care about the game, players who couldn't name 2 professionals if their life depended on it, tired of giving all my money to the league and getting nothing out of it."

Pops: "So what do you want to do Son?"

Joe: "I don't know, but after four years of this I know this ain't it, I'm better than this, I ain't no banger."

Pops: "You want to compete with the Pro's? You want to be a hustler or road player? Joe I love ya and you shoot a very good game but you're not exactly pro speed."

Joe: "I don't know pops, I don't know what I want, I just feel lost, just about everything I guess."

Pops: "What do you mean everything?'

Joe: "Everything, pool, Tish, never having money, you know everything about life."

Pops: "Tish? What wrong with her? Thought you guys were OK."

Joe: "Yeah, we're OK pops, I guess, just be nice to get more out of a relationship then watching her watch TV or playing with her phone all day. Take her out to the movies or she comes with me to league night and I'll bet she spends more than half of her time on her phone. She don't like to do shit, boring is an understatement. And she has no appreciation for what I do on the table."

Pops: "Yeah a lot of people don't get pool especially if they don't play it."

Joe: "It ain't just the pool pops, she just boring. She wasn't like this when we first started going out, she was all adventurous then."

Pops: "That's typical son, people always make more of an effort in the beginning and eventually one or the other starts to do less and it rolls down hill, each one blaming the other, then boom, routine and you're in a resentment rut."

Joe: "Yeah, and that's where I'm at, in a rut. I need a change, maybe get out of league and play in a major tournament or something."

Pops: "I really don't think you're ready for something like that and I'm sorry Joe but we don't have a lot of money, I can't afford to send you to a major tournament."

Joe: "I know we don't have the money but why don't you think I'm ready?'

Pops: "Joe, I've played a lot of Pro players in my day, you have to know the rails and you have to control your emotions, you don't do either. First time someone slops a ball in on you or gets a lucky leave you gonna lose your shit just like you do on league night. First time you face a defensive minded Pro you gonna get frustrated and want to quit playing. You're a good league player son but that don't translate to Pro level pool."

Joe, looking down and ashamed: "Thanks for believing in me pops."

Pops: "Joe, I'm just being honest, I only said you weren't ready I didn't say you couldn't get ready."

Joe: "So how do I get ready, who around here can teach me and for free?"

Pops: "I don't know son, I haven't ever given this much thought, gonna have to let me give it a think."

Joe: "Well, your girl gonna be here in a half hour or so and I'm sure you want to shower so I'm gonna head out for a bit maybe see if Tish isn't too busy with Candy Crush."

Pops: "Why don't you take the bus across town to The
Shark Club, they always got some top shooters in there,
maybe watch them see if you can pick up on anything."
Joe: "Can I take the van?"
Pops: "It needs gas, just thought it'd be cheaper to take the
bus."
Joe: "Yeah it would. Thanks pops."

10:58, a gentle knock at the door

"It's open." Pops shouts as he finishes picking up the living
room.
The girlfriend walks in and seductively approaches him
"Take my coat off." She says
He unbuttons the long coat and slides it off her shoulders
and it falls to the floor exposing her outfit which is nothing
more than a white see through bra and panties set with thigh
high stockings. "Sweet Jesus." Joe exclaims.
She backs Joe up and pushes him to the couch. She kisses
his neck and works her way down. After a few minutes she
straddles him and pushes his hand inside her panties.
"Do you feel how wet I am, how swollen I am." She says as
she removes her bra. "I need some dick and you're not
growing, am I doing something wrong?"
Joe: "No baby, guess I'm just a little concerned about Joe
right now."
She moves to lie next to him her hand entertaining his groin.
"He still mad 'cuz of me?" She asks

Pops: "No, he's just kind of stuck in life, he isn't having any fun and he ain't got much confidence in anything."

"Well…" she replies "I have a girlfriend who can give him all the fun he can handle."

Pops: "No, that's not really what I mean. I mean yeah he's not happy with his girlfriend but I think it's more about wanting to reach the next level in his pool game."

"Oh" She replies "I don't know much about pool but I thought you said you played professionally?"

Pops: "No, I gambled against Pro's but didn't play professionally."

"Well," she says rubbing her large firm breasts against his chest "why not have one of those Pro's help him?"

Pops: "Ain't no Pro gonna help him for free and most are too busy traveling anyway."

She continues stroking him "I'm sure the guys you played 30 years ago aren't traveling much anymore, you must have some connections. How do the old players make a living, don't they write books and teach, one of them gotta understand your situation."

Joe thought about it for a second and it was like a light went off in his head, his eyes got huge and a smile came to his face. "Oh my God that's it, The Priest, you're a genius!"

"Oh baby, we getting a reaction now, don't stop talking" She said

Pops: "The Priest, I played him decades ago and he wrote a book, I seen it a couple years ago."

She re-straddles him and slowly guides him inside her

"Mmmhmmm, keep talking." She says

Pops: "Uhhh, you making it hard to think."

She giggles "Good, it's my job to make it hard, you got it figured out then?"

Pops: "I don't know, maybe, money might still be an issue."

Continuing to grind on him she asks "How much you need?"

Pops: "I'm not sure, enough for a road trip to Michigan and back."

She bends sideways and grabs her purse, she reaches inside and pulls out a wad of money. "Here's two hundred but you take me with you, I ain't never been out of Chicago."

Pops: "I don't know how long we'd be gone, could be a day or a month, I don't know if this is a good idea, don't even know if he's still around."

"Hand me my phone baby." She says still grinding on him

Pops reaches over to the table and gets her phone.

"The Priest, right?" She asks

Pops replies pushing himself into her and massaging her large firm breasts: "Yeah."

She types on her phone for a second then turns the phone to Pops: "This guy?" She asks

Pops: "Damn baby, yeah that's him."

She replies "Everybody on social media baby. Let's see what his profile says. Lives in Michigan, author, owns a pool hall called T.J.'s in Jackson, not married, and active 10

8

minutes ago. Hmmm, kind of sexy looking for an older white guy. Want me to send him a message?"

Pops: "Yeah, that'd be great but I wouldn't know what to say."

Handing Joe her phone she says "Here, my mouth is bored, you figure out what to say and message him, just type in the box and click send."

Joe thinks about it for a minute as his hand rides the back of her head then he starts typing "Sir, you won't remember me but we played a match many, many years ago in Chicago. My son has high ambitions in the sport of pool but needs help. I was wondering if you had time to work with him. Joe"

Pops: "Ok, I sent it"

She looks up at him "Cool, now take me on the balcony, I want an audience."

Joe: "Damn girl, you are freaky aren't ya?"

She replies "You have no idea."

It's about 3a.m. when little Joe makes it home.

Joe: "Hey pops, you still up?"

Pops: "Have a seat son, we need to talk."

Joe: "Everything OK pops?"

Pops: "Yeah. You learn anything tonight?"

Joe: "Not really. Tish met me at the pool hall and I watched the players she watched her phone. I'd say something to her, she'd say something back, I'd say something else and

9

that'd be the end of the conversation, it's getting really old really quick."

Pops: "Look son, I live with a lot of regrets. I regret that your mother went to the liquor store instead of me. I regret not being able to provide you with everything you wanted. I regret…"

Joe interrupts: "Pops, if this is about the girls I told you it really doesn't…"

Pops interrupts kind of laughing: "No, I don't regret the girls Joe, that's about what I need, it has nothing to do with you. The point I was getting to is that I think I can give you something that you want."

Joe: "What's that?"

Pops: "You up for a road trip?"

Joe: "Oh hell yeah but can we afford that."

Pops: "It's not going to cost alot and we've already got the money."

Joe: "We've? You mean you and her? She wants to go?"

Pops: "Yeah, she's got some money to put with mine, enough for gas, and food for awhile, hotel for a couple nights, we can sleep in the van if we have to."

Joe: "You really think the Scooby van will make it, damn thing is what, 40 years old?"

Pops laughing: "Quit calling it the Scooby van, it's more A-Team."

Joe in a Scooby voice: "Ok Raggy, Rooby dooby doo!"

Pops: "You're an ass. Get some sleep, I'd like to leave about noon."

Joe: "Ok. Your girl still here?"
Pops: "Umm, no, she wanted to go home and pack and tell her mom she might not be home for a few days, she'll be back in the morning."
Joe: "Oh I'm sure her mom is gonna love that. Who are we going to see anyway?"
Pops: "I'll tell ya on the way, you need to go get some sleep you look beat."
Joe: "Alright, but I'm not sure I'll be able to sleep, you got me all excited."

It's about 1030 in the morning, Joe and Pops are up and dressed, packing some bags for the trip. A loud knock on the door and little Joe answers it to find a rather ample Woman with her hands on her hips "Are you the young man wanting to take my little girl to see some pool instructor?" Little Joe looks to his dad very confused then looks back at the woman. To the left of her is his Dad's girlfriend dressed in a very mini mini-skirt and spaghetti strap top, slightly moving her head up and down signaling him what to say.

Joe: "Ummm, yeah."
"Well I don't know you, you could be some serial killer or lunatic wanting to kidnap her and sell her as a sex slave. Get over here and stand with her, I want your picture. She don't answer my texts I'ma have the cops all on your ass." Pops emerges from the bathroom "I'm going too ma'am, she won't be alone and nothing will happen to her."

"Well I don't know you either you could be in on it, I see this shit on the news all the damn time. You look familiar, what you do for a living?"

"Handyman" Joe replies

"Yeah" she says "I think you did the flooring in my kitchen about 4 years ago."

Pops: "Was that a gray Pergo?"

"Yeah, that was you wasn't it?" She replies

Pops: "Yes ma'am, but, I don't remember you talking about a daughter back then."

"Oh she wasn't living with me back then, she was living with her daddy on the East side but he ain't nothing but a drunk and she got tired of looking after him. She moved back with me about a year ago. How long your boy been dating her?" She asks

Pops: "Oh just a couple of weeks I guess."

"That's it?" She turns to her daughter "You want to travel with this guy only knowing him 2 weeks? Are you out your mind?"

"I'm 18 momma, it's a chance to see something other than Chicago." She replies

"Alright girl but you better stay in touch." She turns to look at little Joe "And I got your picture, anything happens to her and I'm holding you responsible."

Pops: "Ma'am, If Joe has to stay longer than a week I'll bring her back with me if that makes you feel any better."

"It don't." She replied, She looks at her daughter, and shakes her head a bit "And why ain't you wearin' a bra girl,

12

got your nipples all out and shit."

Daughter: "I like my nipples, he likes my nipples, what the problem is?"

Mother: "Not everybody wants to see your nipples girl."

Daughter: "Then everybody can look away can't they, they can mind they own damn business."

Mother shakes a finger at her "You better answer when I call you, I don't care how old ya are, you still my baby." She walks away and down the stairs. "Damn girl goin' cross country lookin' like a hooker, gonna be the death of me."

Little Joe looks at his pops.

Pops: "I guess the cats' out of the bag huh?"

Joe: "Who are we going to see pops?"

Pops: "I'll tell you on the way, we need to get the van packed."

Little Joe looks at the girlfriend and says "Put my ass in the noose didn't ya?"

"She wouldn't understand." She replied

Joe: "Yeah right, and where you get your looks from, you're like the opposite of your mom."

"My Dad was a good looking guy until he turned into an alcoholic." She replied

Joe looking out in the hallway "Shit, you pack everything you own?"

"Close, I didn't know how long we'd be gone." She replied

Pops: "Well, looks like we can leave an hour early, what do

say we get rolling?"

The van packed, gassed and ready to go. The moment they hit I-94 East...

Joe: "Alright, it's killing me pops, where are we going?"
Pops: "About 30 some years ago I played a professional hustler who had a huge impact on my life. Even though he was a hustler he's one of the few people I have any respect for. A couple years ago I was putting a book shelf together for Josephine down the hall and when she was putting her books on it I saw "Written by: The Priest" on one of the spines and sure as shit it was a pool book written by the same hustler. Last night she found him online and I asked him if he would be willing to help you improve your game, he replied and said he would have to see you first. We are going to see him, he lives in Jackson Michigan, it's only about 4 hours away."
Joe: "How can we afford someone to teach me pops?"
Pops smiling at his girlfriend: "I was a little distracted when trying to figure that part out, but have faith son, we'll work it out."
Joe: "Was this guy any good, I never heard of him."
Pops: "You know who the best hustlers were son? The ones you never heard of."

<u>Priest</u>:

A couple of pee breaks later it's about 3:30 in the afternoon, they pull into the parking lot of T.J.'s pool hall. There's about a dozen cars in the lot, a bright red '69 Mustang MACH I with a front license plate that reads "Priest" sits nearest the building. Pops pulls into a parking space, his hands visibly shaking as he reaches for his cigarettes in the console.

Joe: "Pops, you OK, you shakin'."
Pops: "Just nervous son, he probably won't remember me and I really want this for you."

They walk in and it's definitely a pool players pool hall. Darkened windows but tables are well lit, half the large room filled with Brunswick Gold Crowns the other half with bar box Diamonds. There's a jukebox but no alcohol. Looks like there's a large back room but it appears closed off. There's quite a few people in there playing but it's relatively quiet. It's a pool hall very much focused on pool. They walk to the counter.

Barmaid: "Can I help you?"
Pops: "I'm looking for The Priest."
Barmaid: "Back corner, table 14, can't miss him."
"Thank you." Pops replies He then turns to Joe "Why don't you guys wait here, get a Coke or something, and let me talk

to him."

Joe: "OK pops."

      Pops takes a deep breath and begins walking to table 14 where a very smartly dressed older man appears to be doing drills. Pops doesn't want to interrupt and stands a couple tables away waiting for him to finish his drill. When he finishes...

Pops: "Sir, are you The Priest?"

Priest as he pulls balls out of the Gold Crown: "Yes Sir, may I help you?"

Pops: "I sent you a message yesterday, online, asking you about my Son, we're from Chicago."

Priest: "Joe, right?"

Pops: "Yes Sir, from Chicago."

Priest smiling: "Yeah, I got that Chicago part. You said we played a match a long time ago?"

Pops: "Yes Sir, and it changed my life."

Priest: "How so?"

Pops: "You probably won't remember but you beat me pretty bad, I was desperate and offered to play you for my girlfriend, you refused and left me $500 saying if I was a smart person I could double it, if I was a dumb one I would lose it."

Priest: "Actually I do remember that, it was the only time I've ever done that. Let me ask you something, which one were you, were you the smart person or the dumb one?"

Pops: "Well Sir, I did go through the money in an hour."

16

Priest: "I see, and what did you spend the money on Joe?"

Pops: "I bought a used van Sir so I could get a regular job. It also led me to meet my wife and have my son. What you did changed my life, you might say you beat some reality into me."

Priest holding his hand out to shake Pop's: "That's probably the best thing I've ever heard in my life, thank you for that. What happened to the girlfriend you had that night?"

Pops: "After you left she started bitching that if you were any kind of man you would have left half of what you won, she had absolutely no idea of what you did, I dumped her 10 minutes after you walked out."

Priest: "Sounds like you made a couple of good decisions that night."

Pops: "I'm glad to hear you say that. Want to hear something funny? I still have that van, we drove it here, it's in your parking lot."

Priest smiling: "No way."

Pops: "I'm not kidding, Joe calls it the Scooby van."

Priest: "That's incredible. So what can I do for you now?"

Pops sighing: "My son, he's the highest ranked player in his league, he wants to take the next step and play on the professional level but he's got some issues with his game."

Priest: "What kind of issues?"

Pops: "Mostly mental. His fundamentals are sound, watching him play is like watching you, you guys shoot just alike, hell under other circumstances he could probably be your kid."

Priest: "Joe, Chicago has a lot of good players who could bring his game up, why come here?"

Pops: "Many reasons I guess. I trust and respect you first. Secondly, you're one of the last old school players with many of the same influences my Son has like Rempe, Sigel, Crane, and Caras. If he's going to learn the game right he needs to learn the old school way, not from some of these hack cheaters going around today."

Priest: "Why are you shaking Joe, Parkinson's?"

Pops: "I'm nervous. You're bigger than life to me. Maybe embarrassed because I can't repay you for what you did for me so many years ago. Sir, look, I have no money but any guidance you can give Joe I will work off. I can clean your parking lot, clean the tables, I'm a good handyman too, I can do plumbing, carpentry, you name it, I'll do it no questions asked."

Priest: "I already have employees for all of that. Is that your boy at the counter?"

Pops: "Yes sir, the girl is just a friend of mine who wanted to come along."

Priest: "Cute gal, love that skirt, what there is of it. Why don't you bring them over but you tell your son to pull his pants up first, we try to represent respectfully around here."

Pops: "Yes Sir, I will, thank you."

Pops waves the kids over then advances towards them meeting them half way.

Pops: "Pull your pants up Joe he wants to meet you." And he looks at her and says "and he likes your skirt, sit close to him. I have a good feeling about this, let's not blow it."

They walk back to table 14.

Priest holds his hand out: "Joe, right?"
Joe: "Yeah."
Priest: "Nice to meet you Joe." He turns to her and holds his hand out "Ma'am."
"You have a very nice pool hall." She says shaking his hand
Priest: "Thank you, you have…very nice nipples." Then turns his attention to Joe "Your dad tells me you want to play on a pro level, is that right?'
Joe: "Yeah."
Priest: "Ok, did you bring a stick?"
Joe: "Yeah."
Priest smiling: "Ok, do you know any other English words?"
Joe thinking for a second: "Yeah."
Priest: "Great, then let's see what we've got to work with shall we? Why don't you go ahead and rack some 9 ball here on 14."
Joe: "Could we play 10 ball?"
Priest: "Why 10 ball?"
Joe: "I don't like to play slop pool."
Priest: "Oh, you don't like to play slop pool, well that's good to know, sure let's play some 10 ball then, call shot

call safe."

Priest leans over to the girlfriend "Would you do me a favor dear, would you go to the counter and ask Marissa for a training doily?"

"Sure." she says

Priest: "Joe, go ahead and break."

Just as Joe is about to strike the cue ball The Priest lowers his stick in it's path…

Priest: "Before you break this rack let me ask you something, how much money do you have, on you?"

Joe: "50 bucks I think."

Priest: "Good, ok, I'll bet you 50 bucks you slop every shot in this rack."

Joe: "What? It's 10 ball, I have to call every shot."

Priest: "Well, it's an easy 50 bucks for you then isn't it?"

Joe: "Doubt it, you're a hustler, this has to be a trick."

Priest: "I'm not a hustler anymore. 50 bucks says you slop every shot."

Joe: "I'll bet you half, 25 bucks I don't slop a single shot."

Priest: "Why only half?"

Joe looking at his father: "A wise man once told me never bet all I have because if I do and lose it I'll have nothing."

Priest smiling: "Sounds like a very wise philosophy to live by. OK, you're on, 25 bucks."

Just as Joe is about to strike the cue ball The Priest lowers his stick in it's path…again.

Priest: "What are we calling here?"
Joe: "I'm breaking."
Priest: "Yeah, well I thought you called every shot."
Joe rolling his eyes and reaching for his money: "Alright,
the break shot is a slop shot."
Priest: "Hang onto your money, we've just begun."

Joe breaks the balls and drops one. He calls the one
ball in the corner, a slight angle cut shot with a tough leave
on the two ball on the other side of the table. He gets in
position to fire it in, just as Joe is about to strike the cue ball
The Priest lowers his stick in it's path...yet again.

Priest: "Joe I want you to take this doily and patch your
leave."
Joe: "Huh?"
Priest: "I want you to place this little doily on the table
where you intend to leave the cue ball after each shot, it will
help me evaluate your positioning skills."
Joe: "Oh, OK, yeah I can do that."

Joe looks the table over again and puts the doily in
place. He makes the one ball but misses the doily by four
inches.

Joe: "Now what?"
Priest: "Keep going, it's an easy rack to run, take your time
and patch each leave."

Joe runs the rack but never comes closer than four inches to his doily, twice missing it by half a table.

Joe: "Break and run. See, I can play, and not one single slop shot. I accept cash only."

Priest: "Come sit with us. Every single leave you had was slop, you never once even scared your 3" patch. Yes, you had a shot on every ball, but not the right shot on any single ball. You pot balls well, but you have to because you play sloppy positioning, especially when you use two or more rails."

Joe: "I got to get the table speed down, this is my first time on it."

Priest: "It's not the table, some of those leaves were a mile off. A shot in pool has two elements, potting a ball and getting a leave. They are both equally important. Those who complain about slop in 9 ball are willing to forgive their own sloppy leaves for the sake about bitching about slopped in balls. In all actuality they both have the same exact effect, they keep the shooter at the table. Some hack amateurs bitching about slop are just blowing into their overinflated ego, nothing more."

Joe hanging his head a bit: "I never thought about it like that before."

Priest: "A pro speed player will hit that doily 5-6 times every rack, that's what keeps them at the table running racks. Don't make shots harder than they have to be, that'll keep you in your chair too long."

Joe again reaches for his money.

Priest: "Keep it partner, I just wanted you to understand. Will you do me a favor?"

Joe: "Sure."

Priest (shouting): "Jim, Jim, would you come here a second."

Jim walks over: "What's up?"

Priest: "Jim this is Joe, Joe this is Jim Burnett. Jim if you wouldn't mind, would you play a set with Joe, race to 9 on table 10? I'm evaluating him and want to just watch him play while I talk to his dad. Spot him the breaks."

Jim: "Sure, come on Joe."

Priest pulling Jim off to the side: "His dad said he's got no mental game, let's find out, ok?"

Jim: "Ok, gotcha, mild to wild?"

Priest: "Mild to wild sir."

Jim and Joe walk to table 10

Priest to Pops: "Jim is one of our better players here, not quite pro speed but he can play a little bit. Jim, however, is one of the best sharks you'll ever see, he can find anyone's sharking point, even those who think they don't shark."

Pops: "I really appreciate what you're doing."

Priest: "You guys got a place to stay."

Pops: "Not really, we planned on sleeping in the van."

Priest: "Well that brings back some memories, I've slept in my car more than a few times on the road."

23

Pops: "Would you excuse me, I have to use the bathroom."
Priest: "Certainly, it's up front to the right."

As Pops walks away…

"I really like your pool hall." The girlfriend says
Priest: "Do you play pool?"
"No, I really don't know anything about it. Why haven't
you asked about me yet? Joe said you like my skirt." She
said
Priest: "I do, but can I be honest?"
"Yes." She replied
Priest: "You're probably barely 18, lost your virginity at 13,
come from a very dysfunctional family, maybe your Dad's
an alcoholic, your mom's overbearing and they're most
certainly separated. You like being rebellious but not
breaking the law. You're smart enough to use that thing
between your legs to feel good and get what you want but
not dumb enough to give it to someone who could become
too clingy. My guess is your sleeping with the old man and
not the kid because older guys are more mature and you see
younger guys as busy bodies trying to find their way in life
while older men are already there so there's less bullshit to
deal with and less competition to worry about. He likes you
because you bring energy into the bedroom making him feel
young and alive. I'd also venture a guess you've always got
your eyes open for someone you have more in common with
outside of the bedroom. Your relationship with the old man

24

is doomed because it's in your nature to be openly provocative, he's forcing it, it's a serious conflict making you essentially irrelevant. Oh, and you're constantly wet." She replies: "Fuck…"

Priest: "I didn't ask because it used to be my job to read people, I can still do it sometimes. None of this is bad, you have to do what you have to do or what you feel, it's your life. Truth is though, it's a pretty common story."

"Why aren't you married" She asks

Priest: "I don't believe in marriage. I don't need a piece of paper to tell me who I think is important to me. I don't believe the government should have the right to tell me how many wives I can have. I also don't need some court giving half my shit to someone who doesn't contribute anything to a relationship other than drama. We've given government way too much power over our own lives, they took away rights and hid them under the term "protection", it's just simple control and they have too much of it. I guess not marrying is my way to rebel against the system."

"Are you in a relationship" She asks biting her lower lip and puffing her chest out.

Priest: "Oh yes, been with Lisa for better than 15 years I guess. She feels the same way about things that I do, that's why we get along. She's actually a lot like you, she wears sexy clothing and has a very fun attitude. But understand, we are loyal to each other."

"That's a shame, fun is just fun sometimes." She says

Priest: "Yes, it is. You got a body that don't quit and a fuck me 24/7 anywhere anytime attitude and probably with no boundaries, most guys would kill to get to you, but they're going to leave you shortly after they have you because you don't offer them anything else. Sex is important but there are things outside of it that need attention too, you have to balance both."

"That's why I like older guys all those little things are already in place." She says

Little Joe comes over and sits down.

Joe: "He shoots good, busted me 9-2, I just couldn't get focused."

Priest: "Yeah he can shoot pretty sporty, I'll be right back."

Priest walks over to Jim's table.

Priest: "What's the analysis?"

Jim: "You got your work cut out for you, just a well timed sniffle or throat clearing distracts him. He can shoot, he can pot well when you leave him alone but he's easily distracted. Have Lisa bend over in front of him and he'd probably shove his stick under the felt. He banked OK but didn't kick very well, also, he tried to do a couple of massé shots, didn't look like he had any idea what he was doing with those."

Priest shaking Jim's hand: "Thank you Sir."

Jim: "Anytime my friend."

Priest walks back to table 14.

Priest: "Joe, the next major tournament that you would be training for is the U.S. 9 ball open held in Vegas this year, that's about 6 months out, you wouldn't be ready for anything sooner. Now here's the deal, I'll work with you but you're going to work for me, dishwasher, janitor, whatever we need on any given day. For the next 6 months this pool hall is your life both for training and work. Joe Sr. you and the girl can't stay, I don't want him distracted."

Joe: "6 months? Tish is not gonna like that."

Priest: "Who's Tish, your mom?"

Pops: "No, his girlfriend back home, his mom passed away 16 years ago."

Priest: "Sorry to hear that Joe. I'm sure your girlfriend will understand."

Joe: "I doubt it. Where will I stay, I ain't got money for a hotel?"

Priest: "There's an apartment in the basement here Joe, it has what you need to live, microwave, television, fridge, a bed…there's a laundromat down the street. Now, before you agree Joe you better understand that every second of your day for the next 6 months will be micro-managed and what I say goes, no questions, also no drugs or alcohol. The first time you question me I put you on a bus back home."

Joe: "You make it sound tough."

Priest: "You think being a professional is easy? It's a level of dedication that amateurs will never understand. If you want to cross that line it requires complete dedication and focus, just like any professional athlete exerts. I'll get you where you want to go but only if you give me 110% effort. You cheat me or yourself even one time and we're done, I don't have time for bullshit."

Joe: "What do you think pops?"

Pops: "Son, when you're at league and you have that feeling you were meant for more, well, here it is, staring you in the face, it's your decision what to do with it. You can go back to league night and play with the bangers if you want, or, you can apply yourself and see where it takes you."

Joe: "I'm scared pops, I don't wanna let anybody down, especially you."

Pops: "You'd only let me down if you didn't try Joe."

Joe sighing: "OK Pops."

Joe turns to The Priest, takes a deep breath "OK, what do you want me to do?"

Priest: "Well, for starters, you need to get with Dave and have a new tip put on that cue, I noticed it's a bit worn out, let me see if I can find him."

Priest returns with an older gentleman and approaches Joe.

Priest: "Joe, this is Dave, I call him Diamond Dave, he does all the cue repair and table maintenance around here. We were looking at your stick and we think that's a LePro tip on it, he's going to put a Triangle on it for you, same tip I use. There's virtually no difference in feel but the Triangle is a little more durable."

Joe: "Ok, I appreciate it."

Priest: "Joe, around here we say "Sir" and "Ma'am", I'd

consider it a personal favor if you could make that a habit."

Joe: "Yes sir."

Priest: "It is old school pool etiquette and just good manners. These need to be a part of your repertoire as well."

Joe: "I understand, it's about respect."

Priest: "Exactly. Shoot professional act professional, we also need to look professional."

Joe: "I ain't got no money for new clothes."

Priest: "We'll handle that later, you haven't passed the course yet. Dave's going to go do your tip, when he brings it back down I want you to take your doily and pick out one of those Diamonds to start working on positioning. I'll be over in a bit to set up some shots."

Joe: "Why a bar box, I'd rather play on this Gold Crown."

Priest: "You have to have two different strokes to play this game, a bar box and a 9 footer, tournament tables vary."

Joe: "Wow, damn."

Priest: "What?"

Joe: "Who is that ebony goddess?"

There with the door closing behind her stood Lisa, long straight black hair, dressed in a short black pencil skirt, a black tight spaghetti strap top that showed off her ample bust and a sheer white blouse. She looks around a bit then spots The Priest, smiles and begins walking towards him.

Priest laughing: "That is Lisa, she's my partner."

Joe: "Damn, what magazine you pull her out of? Do all pool players get women like that?"

Priest: "It's not about pool or looks, just finding the right person that fits you, Lisa and I fit each other."

Lisa kissing The Priest: "Hi baby."

Priest: "Hi honey. This is Joe, Joe's from Chicago, Joe wants to play as a Professional, he's going to be around awhile."

Lisa: "Okay. Hi Joe."

Joe: "Hi, you are gorgeous."

Lisa smiles: "Thanks."

Priest: "He's going to be training for the U.S. 9 ball Open and in exchange he'll be doing things around here for us."

Lisa: "Who's that cutie over there?"

Joe: "That's my Pops."

Lisa looking back at Joe: "I was talking about the girl honey."

Joe: "Ahh, that's Kandy, Kandy with a "K"."

Lisa: "Real or nickname?"

Joe: "Nope, that's her real name, saw it on her drivers license."

Lisa: "Your Pops girlfriend?"

Joe: "They just screwing, not committed."

Lisa looking at the Priest: "Bet she could stab someone to death with those nipples. What do you think baby?"

Priest: "She's cute, freaky but young...think you'd have your work cut out for ya, I only had about 10 minutes with her."

Lisa: "Mmmm, I do like the freaky ones. Age don't mean

shit, I was young when you and I met. We're going to need a waitress, Mary is going to be moving in a couple weeks."
Priest: "Yeah that's true. Talk to her, see what you think. Also, Joe's going to be staying in the apartment downstairs, would you mind showing it to him when you're done with her?"
Lisa leaning in to kiss him: "I sure will baby."

Lisa walking away towards Kandy Joe tilts his head to watch her: "Jesus, those legs ever stop?"
Priest: "Careful Joe, we have a house rule here, no drooling on the felt."
Joe smiling: "Sorry."

Lisa holding her hand out: "Kandy, right?"
Kandy: "Yes, are you Lisa?"
Lisa: "I am, how are you?"
Kandy: "OK, I love you guys' pool hall."
Lisa: "Do you play?"
Kandy: "Not yet. I love your outfit."
Lisa smiling: "Thanks, you have great nipples, saw them from across the room. Would you be interested in a job here?"
Pops: "Oh she can't do that, her mother would kill me if I left her here."
Lisa: "I wasn't asking you or her mother."
Kandy looking Lisa up and down: "I would LOVE to work here."

31

Lisa: "Let's talk in the backroom for a minute."
Pops: "You're mother's gonna be pissed."
Kandy says following Lisa: "I'll handle her."

About 30 minutes later the girls come out of the backroom,
Kandy heads towards pops, Lisa towards the Priest.

Lisa to the Priest: "Open your mouth."
He complies. As she guides her middle finger inside it she
whispers to him "She's in. We're going clothes shopping
after I show Joe the apartment."
Priest: "She tastes good, but I still think you've got a lot of
work ahead of you."
Lisa: "It'll be alright, she's got the heart and a ton of
passion, those eyes don't lie."
Joe: "What's in the backroom."
Priest: "A table, and no one's allowed back there except
Lisa and myself and whomever we take back there."
Joe: "I can't see the table?"
Priest: "That table's not for you."

Pops: "You look like you just had sex."
Kandy: "I'm gonna stick around here for a bit and work as a
waitress and do some office stuff."
Pops: "You can't, your mother will have me arrested."
Kandy: "I'm gonna call her and tell her. I really like it
here."
Pops: "You can't afford to live here."

Kandy: "I'm staying with them, at their place."

Pops: "What about us?"

Kandy: "What us? We're not committed Joe."

Pops: "I know, I just thought..."

Kandy interrupting: "Don't think Joe. Last night when I asked you take me on the balcony, you were ready to go inside after 30 seconds."

Pops: "Yeah, I was little uncomfortable, so?"

Kandy: "The so is I need someone who isn't uncomfortable. I don't do vanilla, I like it to be exciting and different."

Pops: "I get it."

Kandy: "Joe, you'll be fine, I gotta go call momma."

Pops walks over to Lisa and the Priest: "Sir, I believe it's about my time to head back home and let you guys get to work."

Priest: "Joe, it's been an honor Sir. Why don't you come back in a couple months and check on him."

Pops: "I'd like that, thank you."

Pops hugging Joe: "You'll be just fine Son, just believe in yourself and earn it through effort."

Joe: "I will pops, I promise."

Lisa to Joe: "You ready to see where you'll be staying."

Joe: "Yes ma'am."

Lisa leads Joe to a door near the back room and she walks him down the stairs.

Lisa: "Here it is, it's pretty good size and it's got everything you need."

Joe: "Wow, this is pretty cool."

Lisa: "If he hasn't made it clear Joe I will. You are here for pool, that's it. No drugs, no alcohol, no parties, you are here to train and work, that's it. This apartment is not yours, you're just staying here while you train. We clear?"

Joe: "We're clear. Can I ask you something, personal?"

Lisa: "Sure."

Joe grabbing his groin: "Why you with that old white boy, can't you handle a brother?"

Lisa starts out smiling then gets quite serious: "Two things. First, you can shove that big dick ego up your ass, that ain't what makes a man, most "brothers" ain't figured that out yet. Secondly, we don't see colors around here, we see people, you better start doing the same, I don't do that "don't trust whitey, live in the slavery past " bullshit attitude. You better get fucking focused."

Joe: "I didn't mean all that, you just look so damn good, you could have anyone in the world."

Lisa: "I get approached just about every single day from someone who thinks they can change my life, or they just wanna fuck me. I don't want my life changed. Priest and I may have a playful relationship but being A slut and being HIS slut are two entirely different things. Most of the regulars here know they can look all they want but they cross a line and I'll burn 'em down...that goes for you too."

Joe: "I ain't gonna cross no line but, damn girl, I'll be

looking."

Lisa: "That's fine but you better not waste our time, we are quite loyal to each other. Oh, so you know, we're keeping Kandy on too, she's also off limits."

Joe: "Why is she off limits?"

Lisa: "We've had a lot of "toys" in the past ten years or so and I think we've gotten to the point where we still like our toys but something on a permanent basis fits our situation better right now so she'll be staying with us."

Joe: "Ain't she too young for you guys? Shit, you look too young for him anyway."

Lisa: "I was only 17 when I met the Priest but I knew right then and there he was what I wanted and needed. When I took Kandy in the backroom to talk to her as soon as the door closed she had her tongue down my throat and her hand up my skirt..."

Joe interrupting: "Damn, I'd of paid huge money to see that. Wait...how can you be "loyal" and play?"

Lisa: "Toys aren't about love or commitment, it's not about raising a family or growing old together, it's just about fucking. It's about having new experiences, new sensations, nothing else, just recreation. Some girl walks in here and he wants to bend her over a table, why would I deny him that experience?"

Joe: "Ummm, because you're committed to each other?"

Lisa: "And that's exactly why I'd pull her panties down for him and cheer him on. Because I care for him and am committed to him, I want him to have new experiences, I want him to explore different sensations, I want him to enjoy life. Commitment isn't a jail sentence like a lot of people treat it, we like to enjoy life and this is how we do it, but together."

Joe: "Ain't you worried about someone being better and he leaving you?"

Lisa: "Absolutely not at all, even "better" gets stale or routine before it's not better anymore. Show me the hottest girl in the world and I'll find you 6 guys that got tired of fucking her. I don't want him to get in a rut and hating life. I give him the freedom, she just gives him the pussy. One's physical and the other psychological, and I've learned you can't just take care of the physical in your partner. Needs take care of the physical part of a man, wants takes care of your man on the inside...and that's where his heart is."

Joe: "So why Kandy?"

Lisa: "She's young, incredible figure, sexually aggressive, freaky and trainable...she's a young version of me, she fits us perfectly."

Joe: "Well, except for her figure I'm all those things."

Lisa: "We've had boy toys before Joe, it doesn't completely satisfy me so it's not something we do anymore. When you've got a couple guys then it becomes all about you, makes me feel more selfish than anything. You're young yet and may not understand this but most of my pleasure is his pleasure. I like to watch his eyes, his movements, I imagine what he's experiencing and can feel it inside of me as he's feeling it, we're connected that way. It's quite beautiful actually, and I enjoy my time with the girl as well, best of both playful worlds. Playing with girls is a lot of fun because they can cum so often, it's a beautiful thing making them quiver over and over and it's much more sensual than being with a man, again, best of both worlds."

Joe: "I know a lot of girls who say something like they should be enough for their man."

Lisa laughing: "Oh, you mean the same hypocrites who drool over the hot fireman calendar in the mall but don't like their man liking some girls sexy social media photo? The same women who's pussy drips over Jason Momoa, Brad Pitt or Sam Elliot? Women ain't nothing but fucking hypocrites with bigger selfish ego's than men. I can't tell you how many women have sat in here and checked out every guy that walked through the door but the first time their man glances at some girl bent over a table she gets pissed. What the fuck? Most girls look at each other as competition and this is just stupid. Let me give you a quick lesson on most girls, we've seen thousands of them through here through the years, I've talked to most of them. Do you know why porn is so popular? Because women at home don't know how to fuck. Women in porn got the outfits, the attitude, the words, the effort, the positions, and they'll do everything, it doesn't get stale. Women put minimal or no effort in the bedroom and into themselves. They throw on a nighty, maybe, and open their legs. No seduction, no slutty attitude, no imagination, no excitement. For being the "caregivers" they're lazy and lame and they only see the obligatory act instead of the exquisite beauty within it. You can always tell how a woman views sex by her expression during your orgasm, you can see if she appreciates it, if she took pride in it or whether she was just going through the motions, the eyes don't lie."

Joe: "Wow."

Lisa: "I don't know how many women have sat at that counter and bitched about an ex-boyfriend cheating or a boring sex life. I'll ask 'em, when's the last time you put on a latex, french maid or schoolgirl outfit, when's the last time you did some role playing and acted like someone else, when's the last time you got him off in public, when's the last time you surprised him with another girl for the night or made him cum on some strange girls chest in a restaurant bathroom just for fun. It's always the same response, they look away. It's easier to just blame the guy. They all believe if they were loyal, cooked and cleaned or worked that was enough, it absolutely is not. Get over yourself. Put on your thigh high stockings, your 6" fuck me heels, grab your girlfriend and treat your man to some fun once in awhile. When people go to an amusement park do they ride only one roller coaster or do they like the different sensations the others offer? Why do women love vibrators and dildos or even riding washing machines? It's a different sensation. These women are exactly why people cheat, they cage men and suck the "F" out of fun and life for them. Your man cheats, you're to blame. You're the caregiver in the family, get to caring and get to giving. Sex can't make a relationship but it can certainly break it. It's the last thing in this world that's actually free to enjoy. Damn Government can't tax you on it, don't have to travel for it, and there's no other sensation like it in the world."

Joe: "I would worship you."

Lisa: "That's what they all say Joe. I don't want to be worshiped, just appreciated, and I am. Let me ask you something, let's say we're laying in bed watching TV late at night. I suddenly have the desire to have you watch me blow three guys at once and feel them shoot all over my exposed chest as they fondle me, what would you say to that?"

Joe: "I wouldn't like it."

Lisa: "Exactly, and Priest would encourage it, and even help me find them. Everybody wants a unicorn until they have one, then they don't know how to handle it, they just expect it to change. Unicorns don't change. When it comes to pleasure with him I can be anyone I want, I can do anything I want and I can do it without judgment or question."

Joe: "Like I said, you could have anyone in the world."

Lisa: "Well Joe, I have the commitment I want and that's all that matters. Some people go sightseeing for fun, some go skiing in Aspen, we enjoy pleasure. I just hope Kandy works out, we've got a lot of things to do and I could use the help."

Joe: "So you consider everyone as a possible toy?"

Lisa: "Of course, everyone presents a different sensation,

no one does the same exact things or feels the exact same way. Doesn't mean I want to play with everyone though."

Joe: "Bet you guys have a lot of friends."

Lisa: "Actually we have a lot of acquaintances, most of the people we know we don't consider friends, only a handful. We take the word friend pretty seriously because there's so many fake ones. You always have friends when you're on top or winning, ever want to know who your true friends are, fail and see who's still at your side. Take homeless people, every single one of them thought they'd have a friend to help them out if something went wrong, they wouldn't be homeless if they did. People are fake as fuck. I guarantee if anything ever happened and we lost this place most of those people who say they're our friend would scatter and never be heard from again."

Joe: "So what am I going to do around here."

Lisa: "You're going to train to be a champion and when you're not training you're going to work, whatever we or Marissa or Dave tells you to do. Dishwasher, errand boy, janitor...whatever. Joe look, he's a good man, he can teach you many things about pool, about being a man, about life...don't waste his time and I cannot stress that enough. He's my world, you use or abuse my world and you ain't gotta worry about him, I'll make you wish you were never born. Give him everything you've got, it's only a few months."

Joe: "I got this."

Lisa: "Alright, I'll trust ya. I have to get out of here though,

Kandy needs some new outfits."

Joe: "Kind of like what you're wearing?"

Lisa: "Absolutely, we kind of like the sexy secretary look, it's pleasant on the eyes and easy access."

Joe: "Guys around here gonna have a hard time shooting with hard-ons."

Lisa: "Pool in itself is a sexy game, why shouldn't women represent it that way? I've been dressing like this since we opened the place, it's never been a problem. The only people who aren't fond of it are the women who can't pull off the look or the jealous hypocrites who don't want their guy lookin'. I do not give a shit what some overweight, closed minded, slob female thinks of me. If she can't take care of herself or take some pride in her own appearance, that's on her, it ain't my problem, and I certainly won't sink down to her level because SHE thinks I should."

Joe: "Those prudes, aren't they the ones that say the quickest way to a man's heart is through his stomach?"

Lisa: "I guarantee whoever coined that phrase wasn't a swallower."

The Goat:

Joe: "Been doing your doily drills for a week now but we haven't said much, just curious, what is the best advice you could ever give a pool player? I don't mean some league player or hobbyist but I mean someone who wants to take their game as a career."

Priest: "Stay single, best advice you can give any professional."

Joe: "Seriously?"

Priest: "Nothing has ruined a good pool players game more than a significant other."

Joe: "Why's that?"

Priest: "The easiest part of pool, or any sport actually, is the physical part. Learning the fundamentals, the reactions, all the physical aspects can be learned quite quickly. To perform them with any consistency, particularly at a high level like a professional athlete has to do, requires a mental focus that rivals all else. Any interruption to that process will negatively affect your performance."

Joe: "I would think a stable relationship would stabilize your game."

Priest: "It would if you took the time to find your exact match, someone who is 100% in sync with you both on and off the table. The problem is most people don't take that time and they settle. The differences that they have are conflicts, even tiny ones, they can still be conflicts and when you have to perform you can't have conflicts fogging your system."

Joe: "Any girls ever mess up your game?"

Priest: "I dated this one girl, it started out great, she seemed fun. The first couple weeks if some girl looked at me it was "Oh, that girl's checking you out you should take her out to the car for a quickie." A month later it was "That bitch better keep her eyes to herself." My game tanked for a month because it was something with her every other week. You can't bear down on a shot if there's any drama in your partner. Tiger Woods, arguably the best golfer ever, his game tanked as soon as he had relationship problems, it can happen to all athletes. It is absolutely imperative that when entering a relationship as an athlete they are a carbon copy of you."

Joe: "What about the whole opposites attract thing?"

Priest: "That's only partly true on a physical level. I'm not Goth but I can find a Goth girl quite attractive and would play with her. Doesn't mean we have anything in common outside of that, in fact our lifestyles together would be like oil and water, it's just not mixable."

Joe: "How much of this game do you think is mental?"

Priest: "All of it. The physical properties are learned very quickly, what is never mastered is the mental game. Some are simply better than others at it and their win/loss percentage will reflect that."

Lisa: "He once told me his game had never been better since being with me. I couldn't live with myself if he lost a match because of me, because we had a disagreement or something, I could never allow that to happen. I understand what it takes for him to shoot at such a high level. We are on the same page, we define fun the same, eat the same foods, have the same beliefs, like the same music and as I told you before as the caregiver I take care of his inner self as well as his physical self, and I do my job very well."

Just as Joe is about to say something a voice is heard: "You ready old man?" A "stranger" stands there with a guy behind him holding a briefcase. Joe looks at the stranger with his mouth open, in awe. The Priest looks towards him, "I am Sir." The three men enter the backroom.

Joe to Lisa: "Is that who I think it is?"
Lisa: "Maybe, who do you think it is?"
Joe: "Efren fucking Reyes."
Lisa: "It is Efren, they play once every year."
Joe: "Oh shit! Is this going to be streamed? How much are they playing for? Can we watch?"
Lisa smiling: "No, none of your business and no. I am going to go back there but you are going to continue your drills."
Joe: "Can I get a picture with him or an autograph?"
Lisa entering the backroom: "I think that could be arranged, we'll see."

About 30 minutes later Kandy arrives to work.

Kandy to Joe: "Where's Lisa?"

Joe: "They're in the backroom, Priest is playing Efren fucking Reyes."

Kandy: "Who's that, he any good?"

Joe: "Shit, just the best pool player in the history of ever. They gotta be playing for like a hundred grand or more, he came in with some guy that had a big briefcase handcuffed to his wrist."

Kandy: "Wow, no kidding?"

Joe: "I wish I could watch. You look wore out."

Kandy: "I am, they ain't no joke in the bedroom, it's amazing."

Joe: "I wouldn't know, I can't get an invite to that either."

Kandy: "They are a real eye opener, very visual, very into beauty and appreciating the little things, I don't know how to explain it. I'm starting to feel them beyond the physical things that we do. I'm desiring their pleasure more than my own, it's just an incredible feeling."

Joe: "So you're digging that kind of relationship huh?"

Kandy: "Oh fuck yes. Been with them what a week or so, I feel 10 years older and more free than being single. They take pleasure just as seriously as they do the pool business. First time I lowered myself on him Lisa laid her head on his stomach and just watched. I could see in her eyes and her smile the beauty she saw in it, like it was art."

Joe: "You and Lisa should make a video."

Lisa walks out of the backroom.

45

"Hey baby." She says as she kisses Kandy on the lips.
"How are you feeling?"

Kandy: "Ready for round 30."

Lisa smiling ear to ear: "If you want action tonight you better drink some water today, you went all Niagara Falls last night, you must be drained."

Kandy: "Oh I will. How's he doing back there?"

Lisa: "He's shooting exceptionally well, you can tell his mind is absolutely clear, I'm sure last night, well, this whole past week actually, has helped immensely. Do you want to go watch?"

Kandy: "Sure."

Lisa: "OK, rules, no talking and no making out with me or him and keep your legs closed, it would be considered sharking, what they do is about respect for each other. We sit, we watch, nothing else not even cell phones."

Joe: "Can I watch too?"

Lisa: "I'm sorry Joe but no, not this time."

Joe: "Awe..."

Lisa and Kandy exit to the backroom. About 90 minutes later Efren walks out of the backroom followed by the briefcase guy. Efren is shaking his head and Joe hears him mutter "Not my day." as he walks by. The Priest then comes out followed by the girls who follows Efren to the counter, Priest instructs Marissa to give Efren anything he wants. Joe can't help but follow the group. He sees The Priest hand something to Marissa and asks her to hang it behind the counter, Efren still shaking his head.

Joe whispering to Lisa: "Did he just beat Efren?"
Lisa: "Oh yeah."
Joe: "How much did Efren lose?"
Priest speaks up: "Joe, would you like to meet someone?"
Joe: "Absolutely."
Priest: "Joe, this is Efren Reyes, Efren, Joe, one of my students."
They shake hands and exchange greetings.
Joe: "I am a huge fan Sir."
Priest: "I was talking to Efren before our set and he seemed receptive into playing a set with you, say for $500, race to 11 in 9 ball."
Joe: "You're shitting me right?"
Efren: "No, we play."
Joe: "Sir, I don't have $500, I have no money and I have no chance against someone like you."
Priest: "I'm going to stake you Joe, I think you've got a chance."
Joe: "I can't beat him."
Priest: "You don't know until you try do you? We all have good days and bad days. Besides, wouldn't that be better than a picture?"
Joe: "I don't even know what to say."
Priest: "Go pick out a table Joe, we'll be there in a bit."

Joe walks to table 5 and starts warming up as he watches

Efren and The Priest engage in friendly conversation. The girls stand behind them with an arm around each other, lightly caressing each others back, this is when Joe starts to really contemplate the truth that what everyone else thinks really doesn't matter. Priest walks over to Joe as Efren talks with Marissa.

Joe: "I can't do this, you're gonna lose $500."
Priest: "Maybe, or maybe you'll bear down on every shot like you're supposed to and pull it out and have something to tell your kids. You've been doing doily drills for a week, keep thinking about your position play, don't make shots harder than they have to be, stay on the right side of the ball. Bear down. Don't be a lion, be bigger, be a bear and bear down."
Joe: "I'll give it my best."
Priest: "I know you will. Efren, you ready Sir?"
Efren: "Yes, I am coming."

The lag doesn't end so well with Joe, he was only a half table short. Efren breaks but scratches, the cue ball parked but an unlucky kick pushed it into the side. Joe takes ball in hand and sets up for a straight in shot on the 1 ball in the corner, he misses it by half a diamond.

Lisa whispering to Priest: "Did you see how bad he's shaking?"
Priest: "Oh yeah, like a leaf in a hurricane, he's got no

48

mental game. I knew this coming into it, we'll get it fixed."

It's 3-0 before Joe sees the table again, Efren plays a safe in the 4th rack. Joe kicks and gets a fortunate roll, the 5 ball goes two rails and caroms off the 9 to drop in the corner, he runs out the rack using the full width of the pocket on every shot but jaws the 9 giving Efren an easy 4-0 lead in a race to 11.

Priest walks over to Joe after he racks: "Bear down son, don't think about who you're playing but rather what you're playing, just a game, it's not life or death."
Joe: "Maybe not but it's still $500."
Priest: "It sure isn't the last $500 on earth is it? You're playing a little slower than normal, trust your instinct and just play, keep your normal pace and bear down, each shot every shot."
Joe: "OK."

Joe sees the table again in the 6th rack, an uncharacteristic cut shot miss on the 7 ball by the g.o.a.t., Joe still shaking uncontrollably runs the last three balls. 5-1 Efren. Joe breaks rack 7 and pots a ball, he has the 1 to 9 combo for an easy win but is a quarter ball hooked behind the 4 ball. He looks it over for a bit then jacks up to massé...not even close, Efren with ball in hand takes the 1 to 9 combo, 6-1 Efren. Efren breaks and runs the next 3, 9-1 Efren. He breaks rack 11 and pots a ball but leaves himself badly hooked, he misses the kick and gives up ball in hand. Again Joe misses ball in hand trying for a difficult leave on his next shot, Efren finishes the set, 11-1. The gentlemen come together and shake hands.

Joe: "Sir, it has been a real honor playing with you."

Efren pointing to the Priest: "You'll be OK, listen to what he tells you."

Efren walks over to the Priest to collect his money, he and the Priest embrace and Joe overhears the Priest say "thank you for being my friend." and Efren replied "It has been my honest pleasure.", he thought nothing of it at the time. As Efren leaves Joe asks: "I have to know, it's killing me, how much did you play him for?"

Priest: "We played for the same thing we've been playing for, for the last 12 years, one dollar."

Joe: "Say what?"

Priest: "We play for a dollar."

Joe: "He travels 5,000 miles to play you for a dollar?"

Priest: "Not exactly, we play our match scheduled around a nearby tournament he plays in."

Joe: "Why only a dollar?"

Priest: "Because Joe pool isn't always about money, sometimes it's about pride or just plain old fun. Good pool players play for many reasons, money doesn't have to be the only reason, that's just what some online hack would have you believe."

Joe: "But the guy with the briefcase?"

Priest: "We've been playing for the same dollar bill since this began, it's very precious to us, signed by both of us on the front, on the back is listed the date we played and who won that year, it's the only record of our matches."

Joe: "Is that what Marissa hung behind the counter?"

Priest: "No, that's just a signed Efren dollar, like the other 5 back there. The dollar we play for is now in a safe in the backroom."

Joe: "So you've beat him 6 times?"

Priest: "Yeah, we're 6 and 6."

Joe: "That's amazing. How did this begin?"

Priest: "Well, we played a match many, many years ago and I beat him pretty bad, he swore to get me back when he had more money. We never saw each other again until I opened this place and he just happened in, but he came in broke, enough for food and a couple hours table time. I made the offer and he accepted and each year like clockwork he drops in and we play.

Joe: "That's crazy."

Priest: "I see you're still kind of shaking, how are you feeling?"

Joe: "I'm still nervous, he is the g.o.a.t. after all."

Priest: "Indeed he is."

The Priest reaches into his vest pocket and tosses a cue ball at Joe. In black marker it is inscribed "Thank you for the game Joe, Efren Bata Reyes." Joe looks up at the Priest in complete admiration as if holding back a tear and nods his head in a humble thanks.

<u>The Sit</u>:

It's late at night, Joe and The Priest are walking the pool hall grounds picking up any trash about. A park bench out back makes for the perfect break spot to sit and talk among the starlight.

Joe: "This is really a nice place you got here."
Priest: "Thanks Joe."
Joe: "Can I ask you something?"
Priest: "You just did. I'm kidding, of course you can."
Joe: "You ever been hustled yourself?"
Priest: "Yeah, once. This little prick in Detroit got me."
Joe, kind of laughing: "How'd that happen?"
Priest: "Went to this place called The Rack. Went in and sat down at the counter and ordered a Coke. I was just watching people trying to find the best action. I was still kind of new at this, had only been on the road five or six months. So, off in the corner in a dirty mechanics uniform is this kid just doing straight in shots and missing half of them. Pro pool player C.J. Wiley is in there playing some quick cheap sets and mingling. Well, C.J. comes to the counter to order a drink and this mechanic who was practicing off in the corner followed him up and asks C.J. for some action, says he wants to play him for twenty five hundred in a race to nine. C.J. tells him he doesn't have that kind of money on him but he'd play him for five hundred, kid agrees. So I'm sitting there thinking; OK., this kids got

53

money he might be my target. Now I'm watching this kid, his stance, his bridge, his stroke, everything and I've got him nailed as a "B" player at best. This kid doesn't run four balls once during the set. C.J. waxes this kid 9-0 and he didn't shoot that well himself. So I'm pretty sure this is easy money. Kid comes up to the counter just really frustrated and orders a Coke."

He looks at me and says "Well that was fucking pathetic wasn't it?" And I responded "Good thing you didn't play him for the twenty five hundred." Kid replies "I don't care about the money, my family's got plenty, I work as a mechanic to pass time, I just hate playing terrible pool, I don't think I ever ran five balls that set, I made it easy for him."

"Well" I said "Maybe C.J. being a Pro was in your head, maybe you'd have better luck against someone like me."
Kid replied "You play for money, I mean real money?"
My dumb ass replied "I'll play you for that twenty five hundred."

Kid thought about it for a minute and goes "You know, you've been watching me play for an hour against C.J. so you probably already know you can beat me so why don't you at least give me the breaks."

This kid hadn't run four balls all night so I thought why not, he runs three or four, I only have to run five to win each rack, piece of cake. So, we get on a table, he breaks and everything changed and I mean everything. His stance, his stroke, his approach, his bridge every fucking thing and he ain't missing a ball or a leave. I'm sitting there in my chair watching this kid surgically tear down shot after shot, rack after rack. Thirty minutes later I'm out twenty five hundred bucks and never chalked my cue. As I hand him the money I said "You ain't no mechanic and you sure didn't play like that when you lost five hundred to C.J." The kid replies "I didn't lose five hundred to C.J., I gave it to him to get twenty five hundred off of you. I had you pegged as soon as you walked in here with your fancy shoes, sipping a Coke and watching players…as soon as I saw you I knew."

I asked him: What's your name kid?

He says: "Stone, K. Stone."

I asked: What's the "K" stand for?

He replies with a smile: "Kidney."

I shook my head and started laughing my ass off realizing he and I weren't so different and just walked out.

Joe laughing: "Wow."

Priest: "Ran into that guy many times on the road, turns out it was The Sandman and that boy could hustle some pool, a pretty good guy too. And every time I ran into him he was surrounded by skirts, he likes his women. I jokingly call him a prick because of our first meeting but we became friends, we share many of the same philosophies in pool and in life. If I had to have a road buddy he'd be at the top of the list."

Joe: "You ever get him back, take some of his money?"

Priest: "No, he was a better player than me, smart money was not to play him."

55

Joe: "Know when to walk away, right?"

Priest: "Exactly."

Joe: "I'd like to meet that guy sometime."

Priest: "I'm sure you will, like I said we're friends, he only lives about half hour away and he drops in here every so often. Hell, I sell his books here at the counter. You can't miss him, always dresses nice like me."

Joe: "You sell his books? Why would you do that?"

Priest: "Well, because they're pretty damn good and secondly, the pool community has to support each other or it dies. We don't have outside sponsorship money like most other sports."

Joe: "Yeah, why is that, where's Gatorade?"

Priest: "Few reasons Joe, players themselves top the list of reasons why though, it's a gentleman's game not played by gentlemen, but rather a bunch of self absorbed, greedy, whiny, excuse laden bastards who don't give two shits how they represent. They'll dump a match if it means more money. They'll cheat and call it a "competitive edge." Doesn't help that the sport is terribly disorganized and no one's holding players accountable for their actions or appearance. You don't see that in Chinese eight ball. Players are lazy and just out for themselves, but that's just a reflection of society too."

Joe: "Jeanette Lee looks like she's doing alright."

Priest: "Ahh, the Black Widow, a cute gal who's flirty and always has her cleavage out, can't imagine why she'd be popular in a male dominated sport (laughing). She branded herself not her game. Sure, she can play but it's what she represents that she marketed, a positive and fun attitude. Ask yourself something Joe, let's say you're a cue maker and you want to really get your name out there, who are you going to have represent your company, the popular hot chick or the whiny online guy who looks like he just stepped out of a frat party? If you don't represent yourself professionally then why should you represent a professional company? There's more to pool than just playing well."

Joe: "See, now back home playing league I always felt like I was meant for more, not just in my game but for the sport, like I had more to offer. I ain't got no cleavage though, how can I convince a sponsor to give me a shot?"

Priest: "Don't, they'll come to you and you don't have to be the best in the world. Hell, look at The Sandman, never played a major tournament in his life but he's sponsored by Brunswick, APA and Meucci, know why? Because of what he preaches in his writings and how he represents the game. Not too bad for an ex-hustler."

Joe: "Why didn't you ever do it, play the big tournaments I mean?"

Priest: "You ever see the film Easy Rider, Joe?"

Joe: "No Sir."

Priest: "When you get a chance make sure you do. It's a film about freedom. Being a road player or hustler is about freedom Joe. I play who I want, where I want, and for what I want...and when the day is over I get to bed who ever I want. I also get paid at the end of a rack or the end of a set instead two or three days or even a week after like in a tournament. I don't answer to sponsors or tournament directors or anyone, I answer only to me. And when I'm not shooting well I can just stop playing for a couple days, can't do that in the middle of a tournament."

Joe: "I get that but didn't you ever want to know if you could be a world champion or thought of as the best?"

Priest: "Pool means different things to different players Joe. Players like myself and The Sandman we weren't after titles or prestige or fame, it was just a job. We didn't give a damn what anyone thought of our game we were just paying bills and it was never anything personal. That's why I couldn't get mad at The Sandman for getting me in Detroit, we were doing the same exact job he just did it better that night. And I'll say this to you Joe, if you step into a match worried about what your opponent thinks of your game or the criticism you'll take from the rail birds after missing an easy one then you'll lose more times than not. Those people on the sidelines chirping, they're on the sidelines for a reason, they talk a better game than they play, no different than armchair quarterbacks."

Joe: "So you don't have any regrets when it comes to the game?"

Priest: "I don't have any regrets period. I think if you live your life your way, not how society would have you live it, not how friends or family would have you live it, I think if you do that then you're not allowed to have regrets. Truth is Joe, very few people actually live their life their way

58

because they're afraid of judgment and criticism, that's why they live with regrets. I have much more respect for the person who does what they want than those who want but are afraid to do."

Joe looking sad: "I'm guilty of that."

Priest: "What do you mean?"

Joe: "Ah, I came down on Pops a bit for screwing these younger girls, been gnawing at me. I tried to tell him it wasn't the girls and he said he didn't regret them but I still fear he might have taken what I said to heart. I was just mad at my own life."

Priest: "Society is very much becoming more acceptable of age difference because sex is more acceptable about recreation than procreation, like it used to be many many years ago...and history always repeats itself. Associating commitment with sex is a gimmick from man not from nature. Yes, you can feel both at the same time but you can also feel them separately, that's natures law."

Joe: "Meaning?"

Priest: "Meaning some people you may want to spend your life with and others you just want to screw, acting one way or the other or both is not wrong, it's just your own personal nature."

Joe: "So, if I want to screw my girlfriends neighbor my girl should just understand that as my nature?"

Priest: "No Joe, not at all. Remember what I told you before, when you're committed to someone you have to be one. If she doesn't believe in extracurricular activity then neither do you, but if you do and she doesn't, it's not the right relationship. Remember what I said, on and off the table you guys have to be thinking alike or your performance as an athlete will suffer. I've seen it I've been through it, trust me, you need to be a carbon copy of each other. Now tell me, why were you mad at life?"

Joe: "Oh, just tired of being broke all of the time, tired of being with a girl who's about as much fun as watching paint dry, tired of playing ball banging leagues and all the BS drama that comes with that, tired of the apartment life, just tired ya know."

Priest: "Yeah I do know, we all go through ups and downs in life, another reason to take the time to find the right partner, more ups than downs. You haven't broke it off with your girlfriend yet?"

Joe: "No, not sure what to do."

Priest: "OK, on your list of things to do tomorrow add "dump girlfriend". You're carrying baggage that's going to hold your progress back, we only have about 5 months left, it's not going to be a productive 5 months if your mind is on other things. You want to succeed as a pool player, you want to succeed at life, don't carry baggage. Because you guys aren't on the same page, at all it sounds like, she is a large weight on your shoulders."

Joe: "Yes sir, I understand that."

Lisa comes walking around the building.

Lisa: "There you guys are."

Priest: "Yeah, we're just having a chit-chat."

Lisa: "Well I hope it don't last all night, Kandy and I would like to get laid."

Priest: "Just trying to build Joe's confidence up to dump his girlfriend."

Lisa: "He hasn't done that yet?"

Joe: "No, I'm not the best at confrontation."

Lisa: "What's her name?"

Joe: "Latisha, I call her Tish."

Lisa: "Give me your phone."

Joe: "Why?"

Lisa: "You want her showing up here one day to check up on you?"

Joe handing Lisa his phone: "Not really."

Lisa calls Tish.

Tish: "Hey Joe."

Lisa: "Sorry honey it ain't Joe."

Tish: "Who's this?"

Lisa: "Joe can't see you anymore."

Tish: "What, that supposed to hurt my feelings?"

Lisa: "So you don't care?"

Tish: "Not really, got guys taking numbers to be with me, better guys than him, ain't seen him in a month anyway."

Lisa: "That's great, hope you remember those words when Joe's famous."

Tish: "Shit, only thing that boy be famous for is not lasting longer than 30 seconds."

Lisa: "So no hard feelings then?"
Tish: "Nah, you can have him if you're into the whole quickie thing."
Lisa: "Great, we're gonna go ahead and block your number then, ok?"
Tish: "Whatever."

Disconnect.

Lisa hands Joe his phone back: "Problem solved."
Joe: "She wasn't upset huh?"
Lisa: "Not at all, she's got guys lined up down the street to be with her."

Kandy comes walking behind the building, kind of squeezing her legs together and bouncing a bit like she has to pee.

Priest: "Door's unlocked if you have to use the bathroom."
Kandy says smiling: "No, I need to cum!"
Lisa laughing: "Girl, you are insatiable...I love it."
Priest: "Help her out honey, give Joe and I another minute."

Lisa kind of dashes to Kandy and pulls her just to the other side of the building where the guys can't see them, only hear. Within seconds they hear Kandy relieving a little stress under the stars. Lisa peeks around the building: "We're going inside to finish cleaning up so we can go home, DON'T be too long."

Priest: "Ok honey."

Joe: "Crazy."

Priest: "What's that Joe."

Joe: "You guys."

Priest: "We're just living OUR life Joe, not anyone else's."

Joe: "That's what I mean, you all are so committed yet so free."

Priest: "If you are honest about who you are and live your life your way the right people will surround you. Wear a mask like most people and the people who surround you could be just as fake as you. I would rather have no friends then five thousand fake ones. People usually figure this out too late in life. Joe for every person that appreciates us or agrees with us there's probably a hundred that don't...I don't care, I'm not living their life."

Joe: "Like the old adage, "Say and do as you want because those who mind don't matter and those who matter don't mind."."

Priest: "Absolutely 100 percent accurate."

Joe: "When did you figure this all out?"

Priest: "In my teens I guess, my dad pretty much pounded it into my head to be myself."

Joe: "When did you figure out this kind of relationship was what fit you?"

Priest: "Oh, I was 18, dating this bubbly little blonde, was living with her and her parents actually. One night she brought her sister in my bedroom, it was the first threesome for all of us. That's when I started to appreciate the visual beauty as opposed to the act itself. After a couple months of this I noticed a big improvement to my game, my motivation, my inspiration to be better at everything, not just sex or pool. The appreciation and confidence I was gaining behind closed doors helped me outside of them."

Joe: "What happened to that relationship?"

Priest: "What usually happens in a young relationship, things happen and you just kind of go your own way."

Joe: "Have all of your relationships been like that?"

Priest: "No, but I'll be honest, those that weren't "fun" generally had a negative impact on me, they became quite boring, this is not a good motivator. Everyone has their own thing, some people are motivated by money, they look forward to being drunk or high, they feed off attention, something, for me, it's the beauty in pleasure, my biggest inspiration."

Joe: "Think every guy in the world would like a relationship like you have."

Priest: "This kind of relationship is not for everybody. Most guys think of a 3-way for their own pleasure, it absolutely is not. If they don't fully appreciate the beauty, the different rhythms in breathing, the muscle twitching, the toe curling, the different tones in moans, all the things that fill the senses, if they can't appreciate all of it but only see the act then they don't belong in a 3-way. It's about appreciation, not action, you experience satisfaction from the inside not the outside and when you have a partner or two who sees it the same way...bliss."

Joe: "I appreciate the talk, we can call it a night, I know the girls are waiting for you."

Priest: "Ok, understand something Joe, don't compare your life to anybody else's just like don't compare your game to anybody else's, you do you and whatever is to happen will happen. Be yourself and let others be, you will have no regrets when your time comes."

Joe: "Thank you Sir."

<u>Bear Down</u>:

It's a Wednesday morning and Joe is a couple of months into his training. Wednesday, the slowest day of the week for this pool hall. Joe's playing the ghost on a Gold Crown and a party of 3 guys is working a table on the other side of the room.

Priest approaching Joe: "Joe, I want to take the girls shopping for a couple things, Marissa won't be in until noon, do you think you can handle things here until we get back? Should only be gone about an hour or so."
Joe: "Sure, piece of cake, where you going?"
Priest: "Probably across town to the sex toy store, girls want to try matching schoolgirl uniforms."
Joe laughing: "Should have guessed, that for home or here?"
Priest smiling and winking: "Yes."
Joe: "Awesome, yeah I got it, take your time."
Priest: "Thanks Joe, see ya in a bit. Keep working on that bank system I taught you, you're getting much better at it."

Joe continues on against the ghost but notices that the three guys on the other table are paying attention to him now, watching him shoot. He makes the effort to ignore them but on a quick glance catches two of them walking over towards him. As they get closer he notices tattoos on their hands, "Nazi" across the fingers and swastikas on the top of their hands. They approach.

Skinhead 1: "Looks like you shoot pretty good."
Joe: "Thanks, I'm training under The Priest."
Skinhead 1: "Wow...I'm...totally not impressed. I didn't know brothers shot pool."
Joe: "Pool doesn't know colors, or beliefs, it's just a game."
Skinhead 2: "Oh it's just a game, did you hear that?"
Skinhead 1: "I did. Is it still just a game if you're playing for money?"
Joe: "Of course, do you play for money?"
Skinhead 1: "Nope, I'm like Doc Holiday, I like to play for blood."
Joe: "I don't want no trouble guys, I'm just practicing for the U.S. Open."
Skinhead 2: "Oh, a U.S. Open, what's that, some tournament for brothers? Don't they have an African Open?"
Joe: "It's a tournament in Vegas where all of the best players in the world play."
Skinhead 1: "Wow, didn't realize we were in the presence of such greatness, what makes you think you can play with the best players in the world?"
Joe: "I can't right now, that's why I'm training."
Skinhead 1 (racking 10 ball): "Well, let's see some of this world beating pool shit you do."
Joe: "You want to play me?"
Skinhead 1: "No dumb ass I just want to watch you, I'm

evaluating you, I'll tell you if you can play or not."

Joe breaks, nothing falls.

Skinhead 2 laughing: "What the fuck was that, my grandma can make a ball on the break, what a pussy."
Skinhead 1: "Well, you fucked that part up, that's one point against you, now run it out, don't get 3 points against you."

Joe visibly nervous starts his run out.

Skinhead 1 shouting to the third guy: "Hey, lock the door for this boy, we don't want his focus interrupted."
Joe: "What are you doing, you can't lock the doors, this is a business and the owner will be back soon."
Skinhead 1: "Play the fucking game, boy."
Joe: "Come on guys we can't..."
Skinhead 1 drawing out a 9MM pistol: "Boy I swear to fucking Christ if you don't run this fucking rack out they ain't gonna find nothing but pieces of nigger spread out all over this table when they get back, (shouting louder) now run this fucking rack out!"

Joe looks at the gun then at the table, a simple 5 ball run out, he takes a deep breath and addresses the first ball.

Skinhead 2: "You better bear down boy, any miss means I get some of your blood."

Visibly nervous but focused Joe completes the run out.

Skinhead 1: "I don't know boy, that didn't look world class to me, we need to try it again."
Joe: "Guys I'm done, I've got work to do..."
Skinhead 1 waving his gun at Joe: "Nigger wants to cut and run when it starts getting tough huh, typical. No fucking way, you ain't done until I say you're done, rack 'em."

Joe starts racking them but is having issues getting a tight rack.

Skinhead 2 laughing: "Niggers nervous ain't he, he knows he's going to get capped no matter what he does."
Skinhead 1: "You like my tattoos boy?"
Joe: "To each their own."
Skinhead 1: "Break 'em but try not to do it like a bitch this time."

Joe breaks and it's a beauty, he drops three and no trouble balls.

Skinhead 1: "Make a deal with you spear chucker, every time you miss I'll shoot you in the arm or leg instead of the stomach, how's that sound?"
Joe looks the table over and says "I ain't gonna miss."

He starts the run, pocketing one ball after the next, playing perfect position...until he gets to the 10 ball. The ten ball nearly on the foot spot, the cue ball to the side of it about an inch away, no cut shot available.

Skinhead 1 shouting: "Whoa, whoa, whoa, what you do there boy? Ah shit, you fucked that up didn't you. Think I got some blood now."

Skinhead 2: "Get that hollow point bitch ready to roll, he ain't making any shot here."

Skinhead 1: "What you think, head shot? Scatter nigger brain all over this mother fucker?"

Skinhead 2: "Fuck yeah, we'll be long gone before anyone even knew."

Skinhead 1 placing the gun firmly on Joe's temple: "What you think boy, think this shot is worth your life? Told you I like to play for blood, now I want to play for keeps."

Joe: "What you want from me Sir..."

Skinhead 1 "Oh, niggers life in danger now it's "Sir". I want you to make the fucking ball boy, call your shot, but I wouldn't miss it if I were you 'cuz if you do you'll never have to worry about missing again."

Joe: "I would play safe in this..."

Skinhead 1: "Mother fucker you're pissing me off now, call your pocket or I'm just going to end this shit right now, I got other things to do."

Sweat starting to roll down his face Joe looks over the shot, measures it out like he was taught and calls the back corner pocket. He gets in his stance and addresses the ball...

Skinhead 1 again places the gun on Joe's temple: "Miss it and make my day, you wouldn't be my first."
Joe: "I can't shoot like this, please, my Mother was killed by a gunman."
Skinhead 1 whispering: "You got no choice boy, sorry, not sorry."

Joe remembers The Priests words, "bear down on the shot, not what isn't the shot." Joe feels his fundamentals, focuses on the task and fires...the 10 ball falls center pocket, the cue ball rests mid-table. Joe looks at the gunman.

Skinhead 1 looks Joe up and down and shouts: "We good?"

The backroom door opens slowly and the Priest appears: "We're good."

Joe: "What. The. Fuck?"

The Priest shakes the hands of all three of the skinheads and hands them all wash cloths, they proceed to wipe the tattoos from their hands.

Skinhead 1 approaching Joe and holding his hand out: "You shoot a fantastic game Joe, I hope you do really well at the U.S. Open, you got the best teacher around. By the way it wasn't loaded, I wouldn't risk that."

Joe shakes his hand but remains in shock looking around at all 4 men.

Skinhead 2 approaching Joe and holding his hand out: "I can't believe you made that 10 ball, that was fucking hot man, good luck to you Sir."

Skinhead 3 approaches Joe holding his hand out: "I'm just the door lock guy, I don't know shit about pool but you were fun to watch, give 'em hell in Vegas."
Joe looks to the Priest: "Son of a bitch, I pissed my pants, I literally pissed my pants, I have piss running down my leg and into my shoe, I may have even shit myself I don't know, I have no feeling in my body except I can feel warm piss. Why, why would you do that to me?"
Priest smiling: "I've seen many matches lost to nerves and pressure. Joe, you will never be that nervous, you will never be that scared again when it comes to this game, you will never feel that kind of pressure. You just shot under the kind of pressure that will never be experienced by another pool player and you shot amazing. You went all "Big Bear" on them and got it done. Pool is never about your life, it IS just a game but with the ultimate prize on the line, you, Sir, got it done. In your career you will play for lots of money, none of it will be equal to what you just went through, now it will all be just a breeze."

72

Joe: "Sir, my nuts are still shaking."

Priest: "The confidence you just gained will be worth all the ball pain, I promise. Go get cleaned up and meet me back here in an hour. Hey, Joe?"

Joe: "Yes Sir?"

Priest: "I'm very proud of you."

Joe smiling: "Thank you sir. Please forgive me if my feet squish when I walk."

Joe retires to the basement, showers, eats and returns an hour later as directed. Priest is nowhere to be found but Lisa and Kandy are sitting in a booth near table 14. They're dressed in matching schoolgirl outfits, white thigh high stockings, 6" heels, both with their erect nipples testing the strength of the fabric.

Joe: "Where's the Priest?"

Lisa: "Out."

Joe: "Love the outfits, you girls finally decide to give into the Joe charm?"

Lisa: "Ummm no, never, but we all felt you deserve a reward for shooting under the gun so to speak."

Joe laughing: "Nothing so to speak about it, I literally had to shoot under the gun."

Lisa laughing: "Yeah I know, but we have a couple of other problems, you have sharking issues and Kandy's in a wanting to be watched mood, so I'm going to use this time to kill two birds with one stone."

Joe: "What do you mean?"

73

Lisa: "Well, Joe, we're going to sit over here and play with each other and you're going to run 9 ball racks against the ghost, without ball in hand."

Kandy: "When you miss, we stop. The more racks you can run the more orgasms we can have, get it?"

Joe: "Oh damn."

Lisa: "Get to racking Joe we ain't got all night."

Lisa sits next to Kandy as Joe breaks the first rack. The girls embrace immediately. He watches as Kandy massages Lisa's breasts, Lisa's hand slowly slides up Kandy's stocking covered leg, he knows when Lisa hits the sweet spot under her skirt, Kandy takes a deep breath and her head tilts back as she moans.

Lisa: "Keep shooting Joe."

Joe continues firing away glancing at the girls after every shot, he sees Kandy grind on Lisa's hand as she kisses Lisa's neck. Lisa's hand still blocks his view but his imagination is working overtime as he continues potting balls, Kandy looks at him as she slides her hand up Lisa's skirt: "More Joe, I need more, don't you dare miss." Joe continues shooting, 4 racks down, both girls have cum at least twice, their moans fill the empty pool hall, 5 racks down, the girls continue more aggressively, 6 racks, 7 racks, Joe's blood pressure is through the roof but his focus is beyond on point. 8 racks...but hooks himself badly on the 7 ball...

Kandy: "Make it Joe, I'm close again, please don't make her stop."

He has only one shot, massé.

Lisa: "Come on Joe, think she's gonna squirt big time here, I can feel it coming."

Both of the girls watch him as they continue playing with each other, Joe sets up for the shot...and misses...badly. As promised, the girls quit immediately.

Kandy: "Fuck."
Lisa: "Huh. When's the last time you ran a 7-pack Joe?"
Joe: "I never have, never ran a 4 pack for that matter."
Lisa: "Why did you hook yourself on the 7?"
Joe: "I didn't bear down on the shot."
Lisa as she takes Kandy's hand: "Good man, you're learning."
Joe: "Where are you going?"
Lisa: "Backroom, you don't really think I'd leave her hanging like that do you? I told you once before, I do my job very well."
Joe: "Thanks for the show, it was...breathtaking."
Lisa: "If it helps you in the long run, you're welcome, but it's a one time thing. Keep bearing down, you don't need an attraction or a reason to be good Joe, you can do it all on your own."

Joe: "Thanks Lisa."

Lisa: "Thank the Priest, this was his idea, you just have to be wise enough to learn from it."

Joe thinking: "Yes ma'am."

<u>The Test</u>:

Priest: "I'm having a tournament this Saturday and I'd consider it a personal favor if you would attend."
Sandman: "I'll be there my friend."

It's a Thursday afternoon, Joe is working with Dave, they're getting the tables ready for the weekends tournament. Kandy is behind the counter filling in for Marissa who needed the day off. Priest and Lisa are in the backroom sitting on a couch.

Lisa: "3 months in, what do you think?"
Priest: "Better than I anticipated really. Joe's game has really made progress, to this point he's stuck to his word and has given me 110%, I think he's twice the player now than he was 3 months ago. He'll have a good test this weekend."
Lisa smiling: "And Kandy?"
Priest: "18 going on 40, I didn't expect that, she's really taken us to heart."
Lisa: "She really likes us and it's genuine, I can feel it."
Priest: "I feel the same way, she's been a perfect fit. Strange isn't it?"
Lisa: "What's that babe?"
Priest: "Other people buy homes or cars or old furniture to fix up, our projects are always people."
Lisa: "Eh, it's just our thing, nothing wrong with it."
Priest: "Oh no, didn't mean to insinuate there was, it's just

nice not to be like everyone else. I know I don't say it enough but I really appreciate you, the way you are and the way you allow me to be me, I couldn't ask for a better partner."

Lisa embracing him: "I feel the same way baby, we are perfect together."

From outside the doors Lisa and The Priest hear Joe shout "Pops!"

At the front door stands Joe's father and Kandy's mother.

Joe: "Wow, what you doing here Pops?"

Pops: "Priest called me and said you had a tournament this weekend, so we thought we'd come and watch."

Joe: "And she wanted to come?"

Pops: "Well, we're kind of together now."

Joe: "You've got to be kidding me?"

Pops: "Nope. When I got back to Chicago she came over and started bitching me out, I didn't know how to shut her up so I stuck my dick in her mouth, we've been together since."

Mother: "He ain't lyin'."

Kandy exiting the kitchen: "Momma?"

Mother: "Hey baby, surprise!"

Kandy: "What are you doing here?"

Mother: "Well, Joe came to watch the tournament, and I thought I'd come keep him company and check on you. See you still dressin' slutty, a little classier but still slutty, and still ain't wearin' no bra."

Kandy: "A lot has changed Momma, some things won't." she says waving to Lisa and the Priest "I'd like you to meet those people."

Mother: "They own this place?"

Kandy: "Yes, I am also in a relationship with them."

Mother: "With which one?"

Kandy: "Both momma."

Mother after a big deep breath: "Both huh?"

Kandy: "Yes ma'am and proud of it, you mad?"

Mother: "Eh, your momma got a little freak in her too, probably where you get it from, but you don't look like you're hurting at all, you're actually kind of glowing even."

Kandy: "I love 'em. I am so happy momma, they're amazing. I have them, I'm learning how to run a business and there's so much more I wouldn't know where to begin."

Mother: "All grown up in 3 months huh?"

Kandy: "Well quite a lot more than I would have in Chicago. I learn so much from them. How long are you guys staying?"

Pops: "We have to go back Sunday. Your mother's been advertising me online and lining up all kinds of work for me, she's like my personal agent and calls have been pouring in."

Joe: "Wow pops, sounds like you guys have been doing great."

Pops: "Well, we've been living Joe and getting by, I think

that's about the best we can ask for. Priest said your game has come a long way but says you've got a real test this weekend against some top shooters, you ready for it?"
Joe: "I think so. Oh my God, I have to show you something, I'll be right back."

Lisa and The Priest make their way over and greet everyone, Kandy comes out from behind the counter and kisses both of them. "Momma, this is my World, the Priest and Lisa."
Mother: "Nice to meet you both, looks like you've had quite an impact on my little girl."
Lisa: "She's had one on us as well, her heart is beyond her years."
Joe: "Dad, look." he says handing his father the signed cue ball.
Pops: "Thanks for the game Joe, Efren Bata Reyes. Are you shitting me?"
Joe: "No Sir, I played Efren Reyes right here in this pool hall. He kicked my ass but it was amazing."
Pops laughing: "That is incredible Joe, you have to tell me all about it sometime. Who are you playing this weekend?"
Joe: "I'm not sure, I only know of a few locals signed up, but with $3,000 added I'm sure there will be plenty of good players."
Pops: "You'll do great son, Priest sure spoke highly of your progress."
Joe: "I hope so."
Pops: "Hey, we're not going to hang around here long and

be in your way, just wanted to drop in and let you know we'll be around this weekend."

Joe: "What are you guys doing tonight and tomorrow."

Pops: "Told her we'd go to Potter's Park, maybe hit the Detroit Zoo, do some other sight seeing, don't worry, we'll be here bright and early Saturday."

Joe: "Sounds great Pops."

Saturday morning rolls around and players start to file in one by one.

Priest: "Nervous?"

Joe: "Nah, just a game, ain't life or death."

Priest: "Good man. Joe, you've been a great student the past 3 months, thank you for living up to your word."

Joe: "Shit, thank you for being an amazing teacher, I feel like a completely different player...and person, I ain't hating life anymore."

Lisa: "We're not done with you yet, come here Joe."

Joe: "What's she talking about?"

Priest: "Just follow her, I'm right behind you."

The three of them walk to table 14 where Kandy is sitting in the booth, as they approach the table Kandy lifts a wrapped gift from her lap.

Lisa: "This is for you Joe, a small token of our appreciation for the effort you've put in on the table."

Joe: "Wow, I don't know what to say."

Priest: "Open it first."
Joe begins opening the present.

Lisa: "One thing that separates the Priest from most other players is how he represents the game, not just from a physiological aspect but also physical...he dresses nice, it's time you did too."
Joe: "Oh get out of here, a suit?"
Priest: "Not a suit Joe, but a nice shirt, slacks, vest and tie. Kandy has another box with dress shoes. "
Joe: "Oh my God, you guys are amazing, I can't thank you enough."
Lisa: "Go change and get back up here and warm up, we start in a couple hours."

Joe darts towards his basement apartment, kissing the Priest on the cheek as he passes him.

Priest: "Did that running man just kiss me?"
Lisa smiling: "I believe he did."
Priest: "Was it hot like when you and her kiss."
Lisa: "It was not actually."
Priest: "We'll make a note of that."

Walking back into the pool room Joe hears a thunderous noise outside.

Joe: "That's not thunder is it?'

Priest: "That is not thunder, but I'd wager it might be a purple 1970 Hemi 'Cuda."

Joe glances out the door and sees the 'Cuda driving through the parking lot. Moments later a smartly dressed gentlemen walks through the door with two scantily dressed women in tow.

Kandy: "Wow, they're just like us."

Lisa: "Exactly like us actually."

Priest: "My brother from another mother."

Joe; "Sandman?"

Priest: "Oh yeah."

Joe: "He's going to play today?"

Priest: "Probably."

Joe: "Doesn't sound like players are too happy about it, I heard some groans."

Priest: "They both love playing him and hate playing him, if he's in stroke they'll never see the table, but he gives an honest rack, doesn't shark and calls fouls on himself, he's the walking epitome of pool etiquette. You ready to meet him?"

Joe: "Sure."

Several players approach the Sandman and shake his hand with smiles and greetings. Joe and the Priest approach.

Priest: "Good morning my friend, come to play today?"

Sandman: "Yeah thought I'd take some abuse today from these little whipper snappers. You playing?"

Priest laughing: "No, no, no, not me. I'd like you to meet someone, this is Joe, I'm training him for the 9 ball U.S. Open."

Sandman: "My pleasure Joe, nice to see another player represent, love your outfit."

Joe: "Thank you Sir, it's a gift from my teacher."

Sandman: "Outstanding. You playing today Joe?"

Joe: "I am Sir."

Sandman: "Great, look forward to playing you, go easy on me though, I'm kind of new at this."

Joe laughing: "Says the guy who's an Amazon best seller for Good Days Bad Days."

Sandman smiling: "Pay no attention to the man behind the curtain. Where can the girls park?"

Lisa approaches the Sandman and kisses him on the cheek and greets the girls in the same manner: "Good to see you all again, it's been a few months."

Sandman: "Yeah, they've been doing some home remodeling and I've been busy writing again."

Lisa: "Awesome, look forward to reading the new book. Kandy and I set up camp at table 14, why don't we all go back there."

Sandman: "Sounds good, but with all these legs and cleavage out everyone's going to want to play on 14."

Lisa laughing: "It's a beautiful thing isn't it?"

Sandman: "Indeed it is babe, indeed it is."

Lisa walks the girls to 14, the Priest holds Sandman back for a moment.

Priest: "Hey, I'm seeding the bracket how I want. I want you to play Joe but not until the finals but one of you will have to come up from the losers bracket for that to happen."
Sandman: "Ok, I'll watch the bracket, if he doesn't drop one I will, if one of these young guns hasn't torn me a new one by then."
Priest: "I appreciate that and keep an eye on him, I'd like your opinion."
Sandman: "I can do that. You think he's got the game for the U.S. Open?"
Priest: "I think he's damn close. Don't go easy on him in the finals, I want him in the fire to see how he reacts, beat him if you can."
Sandman: "Understood partner. I'm going to hit a few on 14 and warm up."
Priest smiling: "Figured you'd want to be where the mini-skirts are, I already put a rack of Centennials back there for you."
Sandman: "Thank you Sir."

Sandman starts warming up, Joe stands a couple tables away just watching and waves the Priest over.

Joe: "He's got incredible fundamentals."
Priest: "Oh yes, he's very sound."
Joe: "He's going to be tough isn't he."

Priest: "Even when he's off he's tough to beat, he's a grinder for sure."

Joe: "Any tips?"

Priest: "He banks like the Monopoly guy, kicks like the Rockettes and gets more rolls than an Italian restaurant, but the one thing he can't do is beat you from his chair. Bear down on every shot, I've told you that a thousand times, always look for the run out, if he's on it's like playing the ghost, you miss he's out, from anywhere, he is never in jail. He doesn't play many safes, he likes to entertain, you have to be able to take advantage of his mistakes."

Joe: "Gonna have my hands full huh?"

Priest: "No different today than what you're going to have at any professional level tournaments. Me, him, Efren, we don't shoot like we used to, you'll get your chances. How are you feeling?"

Joe: "Actually, I feel really good, no nerves or anything, but I realized something."

Priest: "What's that?"

Joe: "What I need to be is an old hustler."

Priest smiling: "Why?"

Joe: "You and he got the cars, the respect and the top shelf girls, that's what I need to be."

Priest: "Joe, Joe, Joe, it ain't about pool, it's about being yourself, when you're that you will have what you're supposed to have. Don't follow a fake society, lead yourself. He'll tell you the same exact thing."

Joe: "I'll try to remember that. It's 11:00, we better get this party started."

Priest: "You going to be a bear today?"

Joe: "Rawwwwwwr ."

Priest: "Work on that, that sounded more like a lion in distress. Alright, let's get it done."

It's a modest tournament of 40 players, race to 7 on the winners side, race to 5 on the losers side, standard 9 ball rules, no handicap. Joe and the Sandman start putting their opponents away rather easily both winning their first two rounds 7-0, the Priest watches both of them.

Lisa: "Notice what I noticed?"

Priest: "You mean with Joe?"

Lisa: "Yeah, no shaking."

Priest: "I did notice that, we'll see if that holds up in the finals."

Lisa: "One of them needs to drop their next match or they're going to face each other in the 4th round."

Priest: "Yeah, I'm gonna get Joe going in his next match early so Sandman knows what to do."

Like a pro, Joe makes quick work of his next opponent and true to his word Sandman lost his 3rd match so as not to face Joe yet. The loser bracket proved to be a nail biter, Sandman's next opponent won the lag then broke and ran 4 to get on the hill, broke the 5th rack then played a great safe. With Joe watching Sandman approached the table, performed an out of angle 3-rail kick to make the ball and he finished the rack out. His opponent never saw the table again, 5-4 victory, Joe shook his head in disbelief.

Joe makes it to the hot seat losing only 3 racks the entire way. He watches the Sandman put his opponents away, breaking and running two of the sets. A little hiccup in the semi-finals with a couple of dry breaks but he still wins it 5-3.

Priest: "Gentleman, welcome to the finals. True double elimination, you gotta win twice Sandman, Joe you only need one set. We're racing to 7. We're going to put you right in the middle of the room where everyone can see. Good luck to you guys."

Joe and the Sandman shake hands and wish each other luck. Sandman wins the lag, 20 minutes later set 1 is in the books, Joe never got to play. They lag again for the 2nd set, Joe wins it this time.

Joe: "Sir, you play a hell of a game."
Sandman: "Thanks Joe, but it's only because the breaks were working, I never had a problem ball, just about anyone could have ran that set out."
Joe breaks and begins to tear through shots with absolute precision looking like a seasoned professional with flawless fundamentals and complete focus on each shot. A 6-pack later Joe is filled with confidence. This is pool however and

any pool player will tell you it only takes one slip up, one momentary lapse in judgment, one millisecond of focus loss, to lose everything. Rack 7, Joe breaks but doesn't hit the 1 ball square like he normally does and the cue ball rebounds off the side rail and scratches. With ball in hand Sandman makes quick work of that rack. 6-1 Joe leads...6-2, 6-3, 6-4...Joe's confidence is waning watching the Sandman pot balls like they had eyes for the pockets, the cue ball on a string. Fearing he won't see the table again, except to rack, Joe looks at the Priest and slowly shakes his head and mouths the word "sorry". Rack 11, the balls don't break favorably, Sandman elects to play safe on the 5 ball sending Joe to the table for a simple massé shot that would put him out...he chooses a two rail kick instead, makes a good hit but gets an unfortunate roll leaving an easy 5-9 combo...6-5.

As Joe is racking the twelfth rack:

Sandman: "Really thought you'd just massé that shot and get out."
Joe: "Yeah, I don't have any confidence in swerving that ball, it's my kryptonite."
Sandman: "Well, it's certainly a feel shot but something you will definitely need in your arsenal, at least the basics of it."
Joe: "I think learning to jump would just be easier."
Sandman: "Of course it would be, until you run into tournaments and venues, like this one, that don't allow jumping."

89

Joe: "Right."

Sandman breaks and pots the 1 ball in the side but is hooked for the 2, he pushes out. Joe looks the table over but gives the table back to the Sandman, it would be Joe's last look at the table this tournament, Sandman takes the 2nd set 7-6.

They come together to shake hands.

Joe: "You play a great game Sir."
Sandman: "As do you Joe. If I could offer some advice?"
Joe: "Of course."
Sandman: "You had me beat, 7-0, you just got sloppy on your last break and you can't do that."
Joe: "I know, I didn't bear down on it."
Sandman: "Exactly. Other than that, get that swerve worked out and you're as good as any Pro playing today."
Joe: "Thank you Sir. Can I ask you something?"
Sandman: "Certainly."
Joe: "What advice would you offer someone looking to make a career at this game?"
Sandman: "That's easy, stay single, stay offline and don't buy into hype."
Joe: "Yup, same thing Priest says."
Sandman: "Well, it's true Joe. It's a tough game to make a living at, it's even tougher when it's not the only thing on your mind. This game is mentally exhaustive because tournaments take forever to play, it's not like a 90 minute

soccer game, most big tournaments are days long, it's a tough racket Joe."

Joe: "But worth it, right?"

Sandman: "It's worth it if you're doing it for the right reasons. It's what you want to do has to be the number one reason. Play for want, not for need. That's something I learned from Ralf Souquet many, many moons ago."

Joe: "How do you know the difference/"

Sandman: "A need is physical, want is emotional. Your strongest game will always come when playing for desire rather than the need to pay a bill."

Priest: "He's right, the best time to play is when you don't have to you just want to."

Joe: "Hmmm, Lisa said something similar and that wasn't about pool. I'd love to watch you guys play against each other."

Priest: "I'm not playing this prick, he's still in my head from 30 years ago."

Sandman laughing: "It's your own damn fault, fancy shoes."

Priest: "Yeah yeah, I know."

Sandman: "Well maybe one of these days I'll let you spot me the breaks and the wild wing ball."

Priest: "Well how about that, you finally gave in to dementia. You're going to give me 6 on the wire in a race to 5."

Sandman: "Says the guy who smacks Efren around every other year."

Priest: "Efren? That man is so past his prime Lisa could beat him."

Sandman: "He wasn't past his prime when you took his backer for twenty five grand."

Priest: "Are you kidding me? That was so long ago pterodactyls had just gone extinct."

Sandman: "And there you have it Joe, he just admitted he has more experience than any of us because he's older than dirt. Now he's gonna have to spot me the breaks and the wild one ball."

Priest: "Don't you have a Nun somewhere to corrupt?"

Sandman: "Already checked that one off the to do list."

Priest laughing: "I am so not surprised. Don't know how we're not related."

Sandman: "Well, no nuns but I am going to take these two back home and have some fun to clear the mind. Thanks for having me in your tournament, I had a great time. Joe is a very impressive player, I look forward to watching him in the U.S. Open."

Priest: "Let me walk you guys out."

As they're walking outside.

Sandman: "Not sure where the hell that came from, I haven't played like that in 20 years, hell, haven't seen a 6-pack in probably 10."

Priest: "No shit, I haven't seen you play like that since probably Atlanta. So what did you think of him?"

Sandman: "I think when he gets some experience he's going to be the reason everyone demands an alternate break format, he's going to be scary good, he's got a lot of raw natural talent."

Priest: "That's what I was thinking. When he got here he wasn't letting the natural flow but rather kind of trying to force things, all I've really done is fine tune that and work on his nerves."

Sandman: "I didn't see any signs of nerves."

Priest: "He was a bundle of them a couple of months ago and sharked super easy."

Sandman: "Well I'll tell ya what, he didn't rattle when I broke and ran the first set, he came right back with 6 racks of his own, that 7th rack though, not sure if it was over confidence or lack of focus but he didn't bring it on that break."

Priest: "No, he got sloppy on that, then the massé shot he didn't take."

Sandman: "Yeah, he told me he didn't have any confidence swerving the ball."

Priest: "I know he doesn't and that's the hardest shot to teach."

Sandman: "Hardest shot to execute as well, at least with any consistent accuracy but he needs the basics, with experience the feel will come."

Priest: "I've given him the basics, he'd rather learn to jump because it's "easier". I've spent so much time on his positioning and nerves I've let this slip through the cracks."

Sandman: "As well as he shoots I'm sure it'll eventually click with him."
Priest: "I hope so, drive safe my friend."

Priest walks back into the pool hall and approaches Joe who's sitting at the counter, Lisa and Kandy are kind of picking up the place.

Joe: "Sorry, thought I had him, that damn 7th rack break."
Priest: "Even if you don't scratch on that there's nothing saying you get out."
Joe: "I know but by scratching I didn't give myself a chance."
Priest: "Joe, this is going to happen to you a thousand more times, we're not perfect. And that break wasn't your only lost opportunity, the massé you didn't take and you gave the push out back were two other shots that could have changed the outcome."
Joe: "I don't get the massé and I didn't think he'd get lucky when I gave it back."
Priest: "He didn't get lucky, I told you he kicks like the Rockettes, I also told you he can't beat you from the chair, you should have taken the shot and hope your luck kicks in, sometimes you have to give yourself a chance too and not rely on your opponent making a mistake. You can't be afraid to win."
Joe: "What do you mean."
Priest: "When you gave that push out back you were

94

playing not to lose instead of taking a chance, you were afraid of taking the shot and hoping he'd mess it up. You're on the hill, he still needs two. On that Push the Sandman played you not the table. My point is this Joe, though we remember one shot over another, it is never one reason why we lose, or win for that matter."

Joe: "What do you mean he played me?"

Priest: "He pushed into a natural two rail kick banking on your inexperience to not recognize it."

Joe: "Yeah, I rushed that decision, again didn't give myself a chance by looking at what was available."

Priest: "Yes, that break shot was probably still in your head, have to learn to let stuff go too."

Joe: "As soon as I hit that cue ball I knew I messed up and couldn't take it back, but boy did I want to."

Lisa: "Joe you shot really good today and nothing to hang your head over. You're only half way through your training and you have come miles in your game already. This tournament was a good measuring stick to see where you're at, don't be depressed about one shot, especially against someone like him, he can play."

Joe: "I know, but I had him and let him off the hook."

Priest: "You'll do it a thousand more times in your career, I promise."

Joe: "Does it ever get any easier to swallow your mistakes."

Priest: "A wiser man than me once said "Win some lose some it's all the same to me."."

Joe: "Who said that, Efren?"

Priest: "Lemmy Kilmister."

Joe: "Another hustler?"

Priest: "No, rock God."

Joe: "What's it mean?"

Priest: "It means you are going to win and you are going to lose, you can't change that so don't let them change you. Equating to a pool player, be emotionally consistent, from shot to shot, rack to rack, set to set, tournament to tournament...regardless of outcome."

Joe: "Frustrating though when you got it right there and you screw it up."

Priest: "Do you know why most people consider Efren the greatest?"

Joe: "I don't know, maybe because of the "Z" shot or some other crazy shit he does on the table."

Priest: "He has made some amazing shots, but, he's also missed a ton of easy ones too. While he has had an amazing career on the table it's his approach to the game that helps put him the greatest ever category. He laughs off the misses, he's never been accused of cheating and isn't a complainer about luck or anything else, people love that about him."

Joe: "True."

Priest: "On the flip side of that, take Strickland. An amazing player himself with a storied career, but, because of his attitude or approach, many people refuse to place him in that category...of which he very much deserves to be in."

Joe: "True again."

Priest: "This game has gotten easier to play over the years

with our template racks, LD shafts, non-directional cloth, jump cues...anyone can be good today with a little bit of time and effort. Being good consistently takes a little more work though and it starts in the mind. We've talked about the mental game, this is just another element to it, letting go."

Joe: "You know what I'd like to do?"

Priest: "What's that?"

Joe: "Jim's still here, think I'd like to play him again."

Priest: "I'm sure he'd have no problem with that if he's not too tired from the tournament. Go ask him."

Joe: "I think I will."

Joe walks over to table 3 where Jim is practicing.

Jim: "What's up Joe?"

Joe: "Hey Jim. Was curious if you'd play a set with me, you got me 9-2 I think a few months ago."

Jim looks to the Priest who nods his head.

Jim: "Sure, I'll play ya, but it ain't gonna be for free this time, you came in 2nd in the tourney so I know you got a little jingle in those pockets."

Joe: "OK, how much, hundred, two hundred...?"

Jim: "Well, how about for a Coke, maybe a Mountain Dew?"

Joe: "Hmmm, how about a Dew and hot dog?"

Jim: "Ohho man, now you're talking, side of fries?"

Joe thinks it about for a minute, looks at Jim cautiously: "I think I can do that."

Jim: "Let's play son."

Jim yelling to Lisa: Don't you be closing that kitchen, Joe's buying dinner."

Lisa yelling back: "OK."

Jim: What do you say Joe, 8 ball, race to 7?"

Joe: "OK, BCA rules?"

Jim: "Oh hell no, APA, some of those BCA rules are just stupid, scratch on the 8 you don't lose, you can pot a ball and call it safe...no thanks."

Joe: "OK, I'm good with APA rules."

Jim: "Huh, thought you didn't like slop."

Joe: "We all slop some leaves, doing it there or getting a lucky ball in really doesn't matter, it's all the same result, and at our level we slop a lot more leaves than we do balls."

Jim holding out his hand to shake Joe's: "Truer words have never been spoken."

Jim wins the lag and snaps the 8 on the first rack: "Oh shit, my mouth started watering a little more, that hot dog is gonna down easy."

Joe: "Well that's not the start I was looking for."

Jim: "Little advice?"

Joe: "Sure."

Jim: "When you're racking make sure all the balls around the 8 are touching it, any gaps, particularly the two side

98

balls, will let the 8 clear out."
Joe: "Oh, no shit, OK, thanks."

Jim breaks again, dry this time, the 8 doesn't move.

Jim: "See?"
Joe: "Yes I appreciate it, curious though, does it work the same with a 9 ball rack?
Jim: "Yeah, it can. If the back balls are loose the 9 ball likes the bottom corner pockets, if they're tight on the 9 it will usually stay in place. I mean, it's still a luck shot it just increases the odds a little."
Joe: "Makes sense, I appreciate it. You shoot pretty damn good, you ever think about playing pro level?"
Jim: "Oh hell no, ain't no money in it unless you're a top, top shooter and I can't be all that with work and a family. It's just a hobby for me. I like coming down here and messing around, playing the tournaments here, it's fun, if it stops being fun and more like work I'd probably quit."
Joe: "What do you think of me wanting to play pro level?"
Jim: "I think every man has a right to do what he believes is right for him, ain't my place to judge what's right or wrong for them. But if you're asking me if I think you have the ability to play pro level pool, I would say yes. I watched you shoot some today, you didn't look any different than some pro's I've watched play, and you looked better than many. Now, you gonna shoot? My stomach's growling over here."

Potting the final ball gives Joe a 7-3 victory over Jim, the men shake hands.

Jim: "Great shooting, I'll go order."

Joe: "Thank you Sir."

Jim at the counter.

Jim: "OK, I need a couple of Dew's, and we each want a hot dog and fries."

Lisa: "I'm on it."

Kandy: "Let me get it you look tired."

Lisa: "Awe, thanks babe."

Jim looking at Priest: "Well, I tried everything short of slapping him in the forehead with my dick, couldn't get a reaction out of him, not sure what you did but he wouldn't shark this time. He shot really well. You OK, you look tired."

Priest: "Just been a long day, always is for a tournament."

Jim: "It's not that other thing?"

Priest: "No no, "I'm good.""

Jim: "He know?"

Priest: "Negative, and it stays that way."

Jim: "Gotcha. Well, if you need anything..."

Priest: "I know, and I appreciate it."

Jim: "I'm moving out to Colorado but not for another 6 months, you need help around here or something you let me know."

Priest: "I will Sir, thank you."

<u>The Sit 2</u>:

Priest: "With only a few weeks left I want you to work on the massé shot. What you are going to do is work in three rack intervals. The first rack you will do every shot jacked up at least 15degrees and use left or right english. The second rack you will shoot normally. The third rack you will shoot jacked up at least 45degrees and use left or right english. And in between sets you will practice 5 90degree massé shots."

Joe: "This sounds really tough."

Priest: "It will be but it's the weakest aspect to your game, we have to strengthen it a bit."

Joe: "I'll give it a try."

Priest: "Are you getting excited yet?"

Joe: "I've been excited since you agreed to take me on."

Priest: "That's good. Before I can release you into the pool world I want to share with you some of my thoughts. Let me ask you something, you're married to a woman, it's not an open relationship and you don't believe in sharing. She goes out and sleeps with another guy, only her and him know about it, did she cheat on you?"

Joe: "Well, hell yes."

Priest: "There's a lot of pool players out there who think if you didn't see them foul then they didn't, and they won't call it on themselves. Instead of considering themselves cheaters they'll blame you for not paying attention, regardless if you were or not."

Joe: "Yeah I've seen that a lot in leagues, I got so tired of it, no honor, no integrity."

Priest: "Remember when I told you how players were the number one reason pool was being held back?"

Joe: "Yes."

Priest: "It's shit like that, there's a reason the Church once labeled this an immoral game, a label that has stuck with it for hundreds of years. Players tilting racks, gapping, pattern racking, dumping matches, illegal gambling..."

Joe: "Hustling."

Priest with a deep breath: "Yes, even hustling. Players don't do anything to dispel the Church's notions and they will whine about anything, a rule, a roll, a dress code..."

Joe: "Yeah, a dress code, wasn't it Minnesota Fats who said "A pool player in a tuxedo is like ice cream on a hot dog."?"

Priest sighing: "Mr. Wanderone was one of this game's best entertainers, he was however a bag of hot air and for years some people have been using that line to justify dressing down the game. I'm not suggesting we put everyone in tuxedo's, but there isn't anything wrong with a vest and collared shirt, like they require in Chinese 8 ball. If this is a gentleman's game like so many claim it to be then treat it as such."

Joe: "When I played in our tournament, I was completely comfortable in the vest and tie, and I looked damn good too."

Priest: "Yes sir, you did, and that's what pool is to me. It's a game from royalty, a game of honor and respect. Last 40 years or so we've really dummied the game down to try to make it more popular, some of that from players opinions some of it from manufacturers trying to make a buck. The game is very predictable today, that doesn't bode well for increasing spectators. Predictability is not how you gain fans. NFL fans wouldn't watch if they already knew their team wasn't going to score. Other sports are popular because they're not predictable...and they do have a level of excitement. People who don't play pool don't get it, it's like chess to them, shooting a ball is like moving a pawn, yawn. Today's players don't help that cause, they play very robotically and without character, they don't entertain."

Joe: "I love watching the old matches with Sigel, Rempe, McCreedy, Miz, all those guys, they were always talking to themselves, the crowd, the opponent, the announcer, someone, and they took a lot of risk shots, it was fun to watch."

Priest: "Yes, exactly, the players made it fun, and did you see the crowds at those matches, three times larger than what you have today, except for maybe the Mosconi Cup."

Joe: "Yeah, why is that, why such a draw to that event?"

Priest: "Even the Mosconi Cup is only watched by those who play pool but I think the more the excitement grows for that event the more it's likely to reach beyond pool players. Pool hasn't really evolved like some claim, except in equipment. The game has actually regressed in representation and approach. There's something I always wanted to do but never could get around to organizing it, just didn't have the time."

Joe: "What's that?"

Priest: "Create a real professional team based league, just like the NFL, but instead of individual owners, teams would be owned by corporations. Imagine, The Pepsi Prowlers, The Target Titans, The Dodge Demons, The Nabisco 9'ers, The Ford Fanatics."

Joe: "How would that work? Like Bonus Ball?"

Priest laughing: "No, nothing like Bonus Ball, just a straight up team based 8, 9 or 10 ball league, maybe all 3, and teams would travel from city to city, once a week or once a month. Have an end of year playoffs and a championship. Make 5 person teams and limit their strength by Fargo or WPA rankings. For example, a 5 person team cannot be over a combined 3,500 FargoRate, 2,200 for a 3 person team. It would not benefit the game to have the top 5 shooters in the world form a team and just ruin everybody, it has to be level competition, like a professional teams salary cap, that would help build a fan base. People like team based events, look at amateur leagues."

Joe: "Wow, that's actually kind of brilliant."

Priest: "I don't know about all that but the sport certainly needs a boost. I think this is something that would be better absorbed into the general society because it would be a 3 to 4 hour event instead of a 3 or 4 day one like most tournaments. Something like this is easily marketable and would give something for younger players to strive for just like they do for the NBA or MLB or NFL, an actual career

104

playing pool."

Joe: "This is really kind of cool."

Priest: "There would obviously be a lot more to it than this but it's a general idea of what I had been thinking of. There would be one set of rules, players would be held accountable, corporate money...it's a win/win for the sport."

Joe: "Take a lot of work to get it off the ground."

Priest: "Probably a lot less than you think. Pool is already in place, tables are already spread across the world, we don't have to build stadiums, everything's already in place, it just has to be organized, the hardest part is getting the large corporations on board. If they're unwilling then we could look at NFL or NBA owners and see if they'd be interested in owning a billiards team. But I think for the sport to truly evolve this is the direction it should be considering but it will certainly take the right people in charge and not what pool has had in the past, leaders who just want to fill their pockets."

Joe: "Sounds like a job for you."

Priest: "I got the ideas but I don't have the energy. In you career though if an opportunity arises for you to make something like this happen, jump on it. Be careful who you share the ideas with because most won't share their profits, I don't care how much money your ideas makes them, it's a greedy world."

Joe: "I love the idea, I'll certainly be keeping this in my mind."

Priest: "I kind of got off topic here, I just wanted to see

105

where your head was when it came to game representation. You're going to be faced against people who are going to try everything to win, who are going to ask you to dump or dump themselves. When you step to the table you represent much more than yourself, you're my student so you represent me, you represent this pool hall, you represent the cue manufacturer that you're using, the venue you're shooting out of, a history, a heritage...you represent so much more than yourself. Players have long forgotten this. If I ever heard that you were accused of cheating it would break my heart."

Joe: "You'll never hear that. My dad brought me to you because you're old school, that's where my influences are. I don't follow today's breed of player because they are boring and as you said, predictable. I watch a stream and see players in shorts and backwards baseball caps and flip flops, that isn't pool to me, just some hack wanting attention. When you guys bought me the clothing it made me feel like a complete player, gave me confidence and pride. Since that tournament you've never seen me without a vest and tie. I've taken every word spoken by you and Lisa to heart and I've taken no gesture for granted. I feel like I am three times the player I was just 5 months ago. Yeah, I still struggle with the massé but it'll come. You asked me for 110%, I tried to give you 120%, that's not going to stop when I leave here."

Priest: "I appreciate those words Joe."

Joe: "Not to change subjects but I've been meaning to ask,

just out of curiosity, do you like the winner break format?"
Priest: "I do not actually, a lot of players do. Pool is the
only sport where you may be a competitor but not compete.
How is it fair to you to pay a $500 entry fee and go two and
out never having chalked your stick? That has happened,
I've seen it."
Joe: "Seen a lot of player spectators say they like watching
players run racks."
Priest: "Stringing racks is very common though at this
level, I much prefer loser breaks or alternate breaking.
Player participation aside everyone has friends, family and
fans that want to see them play. Some player just stringing
racks isn't necessarily good for the game, everyone needs
exposure. If you have such a need to watch the same player
at the table for 30 minutes or more just watch and support
straight pool."
Joe: "That makes sense."
Priest: "Pool players are impossible to please on a
competitive level, they all like something different, whether
it's a discipline or a rule, and of course they all think they're
right, everyone's opinion is gospel. I really don't like pool
players sometimes so I don't spend a lot of time online, they
bitch about everything, constantly put other players down,
got excuses for days and they always know what "best" blah
blah blah is. They'll blame a single slopped in ball for their
loss before they blame the 5 misses they had. Ego's among
amateurs is just stupid, it was never like this 30 years ago.
Of course we didn't have internet then, you talk a big game

107

back then it was in person and someone was always ready to test you if they didn't know you. Talk a game today hiding behind your monitor someone can call you on it but you ain't gonna get out of your chair. You get to stroke your own ego without fear of having to prove it, mental masturbation. The players to watch for in your career are the quiet ones, the humble ones, those guys are sneaky, but they're realistic about their game and will generally play within their means, but consistently."

Joe: "You've beat Efren 6 out of 12 times, would you say you're as good as him?"

Priest laughing: "Not even close. Though I have some Efren moments I am not on that man's level. Understand something, he's been past his prime for a few years, we both have. When we play our matches I can give a hundred reasons why I win, me being a better player...isn't one of them. He comes here tired after tournaments, I get rolls sometimes and he doesn't, beating someone doesn't mean I'm better than them, just means I probably had a good day and they didn't. Take the top one hundred players in the world and any one of them can beat the other on any given day. Whoever breaks the best and gets the most rolls generally wins. Joe, as a hustler, I only played people I was pretty sure I could beat. Players like Earl, Efren, Jason, SVB...these guys will play anyone for anything, I wouldn't, even in my prime. And as I told you before, I don't care where I rank in the world of pool players, that was never important to me. When you die those closest to you will remember you for what kind of person you were not for what kind of pool player you were."

Joe: "My mother died when I was 6, I'll be honest and tell you I really don't remember her. If it wasn't for the pictures dad had I doubt I would even recall what she looked like. Through the years when people talked about her they always talked about her heart, her openness. I like to think that when I listen to you it's what it would have been like to listen to her. You wear all your stuff on your sleeve, you're as transparent as Lisa's blouse. How you are and how she was thought of is how I would like to be known and remembered."

A smiling Lisa walks by handing Priest a folder.

Priest: "Thanks honey. Joe, I know you think have about 4 weeks left, you actually have only 3, we're sending you to Vegas a week early."

Joe: "Not sure I understand."

Priest: "We're sponsoring you, well, the pool hall is. All travel expenses, hotel, entry fee, everything's covered and if you eat at the hotel and put it on a tab it's covered as well."

Joe: "Are you kidding me?"

Priest: "No sir. You're leaving in 3 weeks. I want you out there early to get acclimated to the Vegas atmosphere, it's nothing like Chicago or Jackson. If we sent you out only a day early everything may seem a bit overwhelming."

Joe: "You think of everything don't you?"

Priest: "I've been around the block once or three thousand times. Here's the deal, you're going out early to get used to the atmosphere and get in stroke not to go sight seeing. We booked your room for an additional 5 days past the tournament so you could enjoy Vegas after, don't get the two confused."

Joe: "Are you guys coming with me?"

Priest: "Not the same day, we'll fly out on Thursday. Ummm, I hate to cut this off but I've got an appointment that I have to attend."

Joe: "Oh OK, everything alright?"

Priest: "Oh yeah. I'll have Lisa come over and you can ask her anything about Vegas, then I want you to get on that massé drill."

Priest gets up and walks away, few moments later Lisa sits down with Joe.

Lisa: "So, are you excited."

Joe: "Of course. How many times have you been to Vegas."

Lisa: "Only a couple of times actually, this pool hall keeps us pretty busy."

Joe: "You guys ever win anything out there?"

Lisa: "Not really, we didn't gamble a whole lot. It was more about sightseeing or something pool related."

Joe: "When was the last time you were out there."

Lisa: "Few years ago to promote his book."

Joe: "How'd that go?"

Lisa smiling: "Pretty good actually."

Joe: "Uh-oh, what's with the smile."

Lisa: "Oh, we met this porn star out there, she was something else."

Joe: "Looks like a fun memory, tell me about it."

Lisa: "We were at the pool hall, I was just sitting down next to where he was playing and she walks up to me asking if she knew me from the porn industry, said I looked familiar. I said no but I definitely recognize you from it, have seen some of your movies. It's Geena, a tiny little Russian girl with the kind of ass that fits in the palm of your hand. She's going on and on about my body for a bit and I can tell she's getting worked up. We're talking and she's a billiards fan and thinks it's cool Priest is promoting a book. She plays a challenge rack with him, he shows her a couple of things, she flirts with him. Afterwards, she comes back over to me and asks me if she can drop by our room later for a nightcap. I knew what she meant by that and I wasn't going to say no because I was horny as fuck too. Now, I've watched him fuck a lot of girls and I loved every moment of every one, but I'm not going to lie, Geena intimated me a little bit. She fucked him good, and I mean good. It was ass to mouth to feet to pussy to hands to legs to tits and over and over again in every position you could dream up from the bed to the balcony. But that's why she's a top tier professional, she's all about effort. He's always had incredible stamina but I still don't know how he lasted 6 hours with her and I, she was so

111

tight and so wet. It was certainly hot to watch and she didn't lay off when I was in the mix, she took care of both of us VERY well. She was definitely an experience to remember. You know, Joe, if you think about it this can be related to pool."

Joe: "What do you mean?"

Lisa: "Geena, who makes ten thousand dollars per sex scene, wasn't getting paid to get us off, there were no cameras rolling, and nothing at the end except a goodbye. She still put forth 110% effort. Even her hair, make-up and lingerie was on point, the consummate professional. For a pool player, whatever is on the line, a title, money, nothing...it should still be a 110% effort. There doesn't have to be a prize or fanfare at the end of something to put all of your heart into it. I hear it quite frequently from a few amateur pool players who say they can't get into a match if there's not something on the line. It's just a bullshit excuse and that's why they're amateurs, they got more excuses than they do game."

Joe looking like he's deep in thought shakes his head up and down in agreement.

Joe: "I will remember that. Let me ask you something, you said Geena intimidated you, if she walked in here today would you take her home tonight?"

Lisa: "Oh hell yes. That was just an instance where I needed to get over myself. We all like to think we are the best for our partners, in any aspect of our relationship, especially in bed though, it's just rarely the case and humbling when faced with realization. We would normally take breaks, she was just so tiny and so full of energy she could just keep going and going and she did, not her fault. And as I said before, if he enjoyed the experience with me then that's what it was all about, the experience and the sensations. As I faced a lover who intimidated me, you are going to face opponents that will intimidate you. You have to absorb the experience and learn from it. You're not going to win every match, you're not going to be the best every time and you have to be OK with that and just take in the experience for what it is. It's OK to admire someone and it's OK to not be better than someone on any particular day. It's not OK though to hold a grudge against someone because they screw better, or look better or dress better or play better pool. And it's not fair to you to hold a grudge against yourself for playing poorly one day. We have to get over ourselves, we're human, which is to say, the furthest thing from perfection."

Joe: "You guys always give me so much to think about. I've never asked you much about the pool world, what's your take on it?"

Lisa: "Pool is an amateur dominated game. There's some sixty million casual players and only a hundred and twenty "professionals", if going by the standard 760 FargoRate. Anytime amateurs run something or dominate it, what you get in return is amateur results. Pool can be likened to golf in this respect but golf on the professional level is well organized whereas pool is a roulette wheel. Hell, entering an event a player doesn't even know what rule-set they're playing under. This is but one reason major corporations aren't involved in pocket billiards. Pool is notorious for self destruction and being led by greedy people. The people who "run" pool always get paid, and well, before the players. I can guarantee if someone like Audi or Pepsi was to put some serious money in an event, forty percent of it would be taken out immediately for those putting the event on."

Joe: "Yeah, I've seen tournaments advertised before where the entry fees and payouts weren't even close, like fifty percent of the entry was swallowed up."

Lisa: "It does cost money to run events, but when tournament directors and promoters just start taking out whatever they feel like, to pay themselves, it's a real problem for the sport and the players lose out. Not to mention the tournaments who are late in paying players."

Joe: "Same thing with leagues, players just pay and pay and most get nothing for it."

Lisa: "Well, leagues are a business before they are anything else, I don't care how they smokescreen it, like "we're promoting pool.". No you're not, you're promoting yourself. League operators don't become league operators to go broke. My biggest problem with some leagues is that they treat players like employees rather than the customers that they are, giving them some crap line like "if you want to play you have to do it.". Players don't join leagues to work,

114

they join them to get away from work. This is a night out for them, they shouldn't be worrying about recruiting or having to print paperwork. Leagues aren't for everyone, problem is sometimes it's the only game in town."

Joe: "You know, it's funny. Some players will sit there and tell you how you have to gamble to be a better player. I've been here almost six months, haven't gambled at all and I'm ten times the player I was when I arrived."

Lisa: "Nothing beats plain old hard work and one on one instruction. Amateurs are going to talk, that's why they're amateurs, that's what they do best, talk. And they'd rather do that than pay for real lessons."

Joe: "Before I came here I was one of the best in my league and I thought I was already ready for the Pro's, pops said I wasn't. I had no idea I had another level in me and Priest brought me up to it."

Lisa: "You have certainly made great strides."

Joe: "How is it you guys don't serve alcohol and have such a successful pool hall?"

Lisa: "I'm sure my extra short, high slit mini-skirts and having my tits out all of the time doesn't hurt but Priest is a pool players pool hall owner. He cares immensely about the equipment and an atmosphere that focuses on the game. Players have a lot of respect for him because he respects them in what he offers them. You'll never hear someone bitch about table drift, chipped balls, worn felt or a dead rail in here."

Joe: "This is absolutely the most well kept pool hall I've

ever been in. When I first came in I was a bit intimated, it wasn't what I was expecting."

Lisa: "People need to stop playing in bars and support the pool halls but at the same time pool halls need to reinvest in their equipment, in their customers. Bars with a couple of tables don't give two shits about the equipment and vendors just care about the quarters. But players need to quit being so cheap too. They'll go and spend hundreds or thousands on equipment but bitch about paying for a couple hours of table time."

Joe: "Plus youth can't go into bars."

Lisa: "In most instances that's right. Sometimes they can up to a certain time but is that where anyone really wants to take their kid? As you've seen we get a lot of kids in here and Priest has worked with many of them for nothing."

Joe: "They are the future of the game. I'm waiting for when pool is offered to high schools."

Lisa: "Yes they are and you'll be waiting a long time. Do you see poker or craps in school? Pool has been treated poorly for far too long in the U.S., schools aren't going to teach students to become gamblers, it's just not a legitimate career choice like football or basketball. Other countries can do this, we just can't right now until we get the sport...respectful."

Joe: "Yeah, I totally get that."

Lisa: "Compared to other cue sports like Snooker, Russian Pyramid or Chinese 8 ball, American pool is lacking in the class and respect categories. I was watching a Chinese 8 ball match and a player banged the chalk on the rail after a bad leave, the referee went right up to him and told him not to do that. Oh yeah, and that was an American "Professional". There's nothing wrong with demanding respect in the game and holding players accountable when they don't act appropriately. We have set such low standards for the game over here it's ridiculous. But, once again, it's amateur dominated and run so we're left with amateurish results."

Joe: "Think it'll ever change?"

Lisa: "Hard to say for certain but probably not in my lifetime. Priest's idea of a professional league might help. It would at least create separation between pro and amateur and give amateurs and the youth something to strive for."

Joe: "Yeah, he told me about that, I love that idea. I better get on my massé drills, I do appreciate the talk."

<u>Open</u>:

Priest shouting down to Joe's apartment: "You ready? Our ride is here."
Joe: "Our ride?"
Priest: "Yeah, we rented a limousine to take you to the airport."
Joe: "Are you kidding?"
Priest: "Nope, girls are already out there waiting for us."

The guys walk out of the pool hall to see Lisa and Kandy standing next to the limousine in matching little black dresses.

Joe: "Wow, you girls always look hot, but those dresses, just...wow!"
Lisa smiling: "Yeah, after we drop you off we're going to wear out the old man in the back of this limo."
Joe laughing: "Damn."

The limo pulls away from the pool hall.

Priest: "Joe, there's something I want you to remember."
Joe: "What's that?"
Priest: "I'm honored to have been your teacher, and no matter what happens over the next two weeks, I'm very proud of you."
Joe humbled: "Thank you sir."

118

Priest: "Remember to just play. Don't try to force your focus, transfer the same nonchalant practice attitude into your match, just play, don't over focus."
Joe: "I will, I promise. See you on Friday?"
Priest: "Absolutely. And one other thing."
Joe: "What's that?"
Priest: "Do you know why critics are critics?"
Joe: "Because they can't?"
Lisa: "That's exactly right, they criticize because they can't do what someone else does. They have no creativity and no drive to improve themselves so they just criticize everyone else."
Priest: "Sinner or saint, winner or loser, it doesn't matter, someone will always be there to tell you that you did something wrong or should have done something differently. I blame the great dividers, religion and politics, it's always their way is the best way and anyone who disagrees is wrong or stupid. Don't buy into the bullshit. You do you and fuck everybody else, the right people will have your back when it's needed."

Joe arrives at the hotel to check in.

Clerk: "Sir, your room number is 233 and your package is in our safe, do you want to pick it up now?"
Joe: "Package?"
Clerk: "Yes Sir, according to this it arrived two days ago."
Joe: "I guess I'll take it now."

The clerk leaves and returns with a long tube package:
"Here you go Sir."
Joe takes in a few sights as he heads up to his room. He lays
his bags on the bed and opens his package. He pulls out a
cue stick, a Meucci 21st Century, finished all in black with
pearl purple inlays, engraved on the base is Joe "Bear"
Williams. A note wrapped around it:

"Joe, you have 5 days to break in this cue and get
accustomed to it's feel, it won't be too much different than
your worn out Brunswick. Save the sightseeing and
fraternizing for after the tournament, head over to Griff's
and bear down and get focused. Priest"

Joe sits on the bed and remembers the past six months then
whispers to himself "I can never repay you."

Joe spends the next few days at Griff's pool hall just doing
drills, he declines many offers to play.

"Welcome to the 9 ball U.S. Open here at Mandalay Bay
resort and casino in fabulous Las Vegas. I'm your Host
Chris Berman with the re-introduction of pocket billiards on
ESPN. My co-host for this weekend is the incomparable,
color commentator extraordinaire, Pretty Boy Floyd, Jimmy
Mataya."
Jimmy: "Thank you Chris it's a real pleasure being with you
here today and wow do we have some action this week, 128

120

of the world's finest pool players all under one roof."

Chris: "Our first match pits pool legend Johnny Archer against new comer Joe Williams."

Jimmy: "Well, Johnny's been around the game a long time, he's seen it all he's done it all."

Chris: "What do you know about Joe Williams?"

Jimmy: "I know he's in the U.S. Open. I've never seen this kid shoot but I'll tell you this, I seen him walking around with a T.J.'s pool hall patch on his back, you know who owns that pool hall my friend?"

Chris: "No Sir."

Jimmy: "The Priest owns that pool hall and let me tell you a little something about the Priest, he knows pool and he knows pool players. If he sponsored Joe Williams then I can tell you right now Joe Williams can play some pool my friend."

Joe waiting for his match to be called scans the audience looking for the Priest. Joe walks to the counter to get a water, a hand touches his shoulder, he turns to see Pops.

Joe: "Pops? What are you doing here?"

Pops: "I got a call from Lisa a couple days ago saying something came up and they couldn't make it out here, told me I had a plane ticket waiting for me and a room on standby."

Joe: "Wow, hope everything is OK."

Pops: "I'm sure it is. Where are you playing so I know

where to sit."

Joe: "I drew Johnny Archer first, we've got the TV table."

Pops: "Holy shit, you're gonna be on TV?"

Joe: "Yeah, ESPN is covering the Open this year."

Pops: "How exciting, my boy on TV. I'm going to see if I can get a seat up front. Good luck Son."

Joe: "Thanks Pops."

Chris: "Well we're about to find out as the players are about to lag."

Joe and Johnny lag for the break, it's very close but the referee announces Johnny wins it. He breaks but scratches. Joe takes ball in hand and sets up for an angle shot on the one ball, he misses it badly."

Chris: "Looks like a little bit of nerves may have got him on that one Jimmy."

Jimmy: "Yeah not the start he was looking for that's for sure. He looks good though, I love it when players dress the part and represent the game professionally, everyone should wear a vest and tie."

Chris: "I can't disagree Jimmy, he looks very professional. That's a gorgeous cue stick too."

Jimmy: "Yes it is, purple is the color of royalty."

Joe sitting in his chair reminding himself of the Priests words, "bear down, bear down, bear down." Johnny runs that rack out and breaks and runs the next 2 taking a 3-0 lead. Johnny breaks the 4th rack and pots the 1 ball in the side, he doesn't have a great run out and opts to play a strong safety on the deuce.

Jimmy: "Wow, great shot, that's what we call putting your opponent in jail, Johnny's got to be really pleased with that shot."
Chris: "So what are Joe's options here Jimmy?"
Jimmy: "Well he doesn't have many that's for sure, he's going to need some luck, I don't even see a decent kick shot. If he can get past the 6 ball he might be able to two-rail kick this."

Joe spends some extra time looking over the table looking at every possible option then approaches the ball.

Chris: "What's he doing here Jimmy?"
Jimmy: "Well, it looks like he's going to attempt a rail jump. This is a tough tough shot my friend, not many players would even attempt it it's such a low percentage shot, a million things can go wrong here and he's got to jump a mile to get over three balls. I don't like it."

Joe snaps the shot, the cue ball comes off the rail in the air and strikes the 2 ball perfectly potting it in the corner. Mr. Archer smiling taps his stick on the floor, the crowd applauds loudly.

Chris: "Wow, did you see that?"
Jimmy: "That was absolutely unbelievable Chris, probably
the best shot you'll see this whole tournament. Tell you
what folks if you don't know who Joe Williams is, you sure
do now, wow, what a shot!"

Joe walks over to his chair and wipes his stick down giving
himself and the crowd time to settle down after that shot.
He takes a couple deep breathes and refocuses on the table
layout, it's a tough one but he manages it to make it 3-1. Joe
breaks rack 5 and snaps the 9, 3-2 Johnny. Joe breaks rack 6
and makes 3, he shoots quickly and with purpose, repeating
the words "bear down" in his head on every shot, 3-3, all
tied up. Joe breaks rack 7, he makes the wing ball but is
hooked for the 1, he pushes but hits it too hard and leaves
Johnny an easy shot and a routine out, 4-3 Johnny in a race
to 7. As Johnny breaks and begins shooting rack 8 Joe sits
in his chair looking over his new cue stick, he looks at his
engraved name and with the Priest's image and words in his
mind his whispers to himself "I am a bear, I ain't missing
again." Johnny makes it to the hill, 6-3, has a decent break
in rack 10 but no shot on the 1 ball and the 9 ball is hanging
on the edge in the side pocket, he pushes to a natural 2 rail
kick shot, Joe would catch that move this time. Joe pockets
the 1 ball on the kick then plays the carom shot off the 2 ball
to pot the 9 in the side. Again Johnny taps his stick on the
floor acknowledging the great shooting. Joe quickly makes
it hill hill, and then snaps the 9 in rack 13 for the 7-6 victory.

Johnny shakes his hand.

Johnny: "You made some incredible shots, you deserved that win, good luck the rest of the way, I hope to see you again in the finals."
Joe: "Thank you Sir, it's been a real honor playing with you."

Pretty Boy Floyd does his post game interview.

Jimmy: "How are you feeling Joe taking out one of the best players to ever play this game?"
Joe: "I feel good, he's still the best, I just got a couple lucky rolls and he didn't."
Jimmy: "Not going to get any easier for you, your next opponent is a guy who's won the World Pool Masters a couple of times, David Alcaide."
Joe: "He's an incredible player too, I just hope he let's me to the table at least once."
Jimmy: "Yes he is, you'll have to bear down if you get an opportunity."
Joe: "My teacher has embedded that notion in my head."
Jimmy: "The Priest?"
Joe: "Yes Sir. I spent the last 6 months with him, I wouldn't be here without him, wish he was here."
Jimmy: "And there you have it all you little Floydsters out there. When you're ready to take your game to the next level get out there and find you a real instructor like the

Priest, someone with real road experience, they can teach you everything you want to know about the game."

Joe looks over the bracket then goes to sit with his pops.

Pops: "That was great Joe, when do you play again."
Joe: "Probably a couple hours, gotta play Alcaide next, he's tough. Check out this stick, it was waiting for me when I got here."
Pops: "Wow, that's beautiful. Joe "Bear" Williams, that's really cool Joe, or should I call you "Bear"?
Joe smiling: "Ah, I think it's more of a reminder to bear down on every single shot, can't lose if I do."
Pops: "Well, I think it's a fitting nickname son and a stunning cue."
Joe: "Thanks pops, wish he was here though."

A young woman approaches.

"Hey Joe, you shot a hell of a match, wondering if you'd sign my program."
Joe: "You're Kristina Tkach, thank you, I'm honored, but you have to sign mine too."
Kristina smiling: "Of course."

Pops: "Look at you getting all famous and shit."

A gentleman walks by and shakes Joe's hand: "Good match,

very impressive."

Pops: "Who was that?"
Joe: "Shane VanBoening, only the number 1 player in the U.S., he's won this event a few times."
Pops: "Don't be getting all starstruck Joe, they're admiring the Bear right now, stay focused."

Joe's squeaks by his second match, against David, 7-6. David, who seemed like he had other things on his mind, made several uncharacteristic mistakes that Joe was able to take advantage of. Joe makes quick work of his next two no name opponents then gets a crack at Mr.Eagle Eye himself.

Jason: "Been watching you play, you shoot pretty damn good."
Joe: "Thanks, noticed a lot people been watching me."
Jason: "What's with the tie?"
Joe: "Old school."
Jason: "Eh, the game has evolved past all of that."
Joe: "Evolved or regressed?"
Jason: "Touché."

Jason falls 7-5. Joe gets a bye his next round because a player had to leave for personal reasons. One more match to make it to the finals, and it's a tester, Albanian all star Eklent Kaci. This match proved to be about grinding. Neither player was breaking particularly well and the balls weren't spreading nicely. Kaci's safety play wasn't on par and you could see the disgust in his face. Joe was potting well but was not getting favorable rolls on break out balls. Joe squeaked out the victory 7-6.

A middle aged black woman approaches Joe.

Jada: "Hi, I'm Jada. My husband and son are sitting over there and my son would really like to meet you. He watched every single one of your matches and cheered or clapped every time you made a ball."
Joe: "Sure, I'd love to meet him."
Jada: "Be patient OK, he has down syndrome."

Joe and pops follows Jada. Jada introduces them.

Jada: "This is my husband David and this is my son Elijah, he's a big fan."
Joe shakes Davids hand then holds it out for her son.

Elijah: "I'm Elijah and you're my favorite player."
Joe: "Well thank you sir, do you play pool too."
Elijah: "Yes but I'm not very good like you."
Jada: "We have a table at home."
Joe: "Wow, that's great. It takes a long time to be really good, how old are you?"
Elijah holding up two fingers: "I'm 12."

Joe whispers something to pops and pops walks away.

Joe: "I remember being 12, I wasn't very good at pool when I was 12 either."

A few moments go by with casual conversation and pops returns.

Joe: "Elijah, can I tell you a story."
Elijah: "Oh yes."
Joe: "When I was 12 a guy who owned a pool hall gave me a stick and for the last 10 years I've been training with that stick. The last 6 months I've been training under a great master called the Priest and he just gave me a new stick. This stick has helped me become a very good player. I was wondering if you would like to have it. It might help you become a great player too."

Joe takes his old Brunswick cue from pops, pulls it out of the case and hands it to Elijah who's eyes got as large as dinner plates. Elijah smiling ear to ear looks the cue over top to bottom then hands it back to Joe.

Joe: "You don't like it?"
Elijah: "You didn't sign it."
Joe smiling: "You're right, I didn't, I am very sorry."

Joe looks around for a second realizing he has nothing to

129

write with. A hand with a marker comes over his right
shoulder. Joe turns to see Shane VanBoening smiling, he
gives Joe a wink. Joe nods his head in gratitude then signs
the cue stick and hands it back to Elijah.

Joe: "Are you going to watch the finals."
Elijah: "I am not leaving until you win."
Joe: "Well, make sure you have a good seat so you can see
everything, OK?"
Elijah: "OK, I will sit there with my new great player cue."

Joe stands up. David shakes his hand, Jada kisses him on
the cheek, a tear on her own cheek.
Jada: "Thank you, I don't think he can express what that
truly meant to him."
Joe: "The eyes said it all, they never lie, didn't matter if he
could express it in words or not."
Jada: "I have no doubt it will be his most prized possession.
You are a true professional."

As Joe heads to the finals staging area he sees a dozen or so
players nodding their heads at him. He's certain if his play
hasn't earned their respect yet that his gestures most
certainly has. Joe and Shane sitting together waiting for
their match to be called.

Joe: "Thanks for the marker."
Shane: "You're welcome. What you did was pretty damn

nice."

Joe: "Thank you sir."

Shane: "My time in this sport is nearing it's end, yours is just beginning. I like what I see from you."

Joe: "Wow, thank you."

Shane smiling and leaning closer to Joe: "I'm still going to beat you today though."

Joe laughing: "Well I hope to at least make it a little challenging for you."

Chris: "Ladies and gentleman, have we got a finals match for you. New comer Joe "The Bear" Williams, who's proven to be an absolute offensive powerhouse, takes on arguably the best 9 ball player in the game today, Shane "The South Dakota Kid" VanBoening."

Jimmy: "I'll tell ya what my friend, this is going to be an explosive match. Joe plays very aggressive, high risk, old school pool and Shane plays every aspect of the game very consistently. The finals is a race to 13 and this match up certainly has the potential to go hill hill. As 9 ball does it will come down to the break and who gets the lucky rolls. I gotta give the breaking edge to Shane though, he is a beast."

Chris: "I couldn't agree more Jimmy. Everything on the scorecard favors Shane in this match, but Joe has gone through some very tough competitors to get to this point."

Jimmy: "Indeed he has, some world class players Chris, from masters to legends. He is certainly making a name for himself."

131

The players are introduced and they lag for the break, Shane wins the lag...barely. Shane breaks and pots two balls but as usual in this game the last ball rolling hooked him a bit on his first shot. He plays a push out. Joe decides to play and goes with the a 3-rail kick and makes a good hit. He gets a lucky roll and hooks Shane again. Shane looking over the table chalking and shaking his head up and down. Shane tries a 2-rail kick, he gets a good hit but leaves Joe a shot in the corner. Seven shots later Joe is up 1-0. Joe looks at Elijah and gives him a wink. Elijah is smiling ear to ear. Joe breaks and run the second rack, 2-0 Joe leading in a race to 13. Joe breaks rack, pots the 1 ball in the side and has a long shot on the two ball, he jaws it leaving a routine out for Shane, 2-1 Joe. Shane breaks and runs the next 4 racks, 5-2 Shane.

Jimmy: "And Shane has caught a gear. There's nothing that Joe can do but watch and if you can't play great pool at least you can watch great pool and right now Shane is putting on a positioning clinic."
Chris: "That chair is a lonely place for a pool player, what goes through the mind of a pool player in the chair?"
Jimmy: "You're praying your opponent makes a mistake and kicking yourself for letting them to the table. I guarantee he's been replaying that missed 2 ball in his head and waiting for a chance to redeem himself."

Shane breaks rack 8 but scratches, cue ball got kicked in the

132

side. Joe with ball in hand has an easy 1 to 9 combo, 5-3
Shane. Joe sits down and waits for the referee to rack. He
ponders everything he's been through the past 6 months. All
of the mistakes, all of the progress, all of the training, trying
to quickly recall every detail. He feels tight but not nervous.
He thinks about Lisa and Kandy's performance in their
schoolgirl outfits and smiles, he approaches the table a little
looser. With the girls vivid in his mind Joe starts playing
more on instinct rather than text book, not really completely
focused on one thing or another, just playing, thinking about
the girls moans and movements. Before even he realizes it
the score is 5-12 Joe.

Jimmy: "I told you this kid had to be something special for
someone like the Priest to sponsor him. What a show he has
put on here today, Shane is just beside himself right now."
Chris: "This has got to be painful for him, it's like Joe just
can't do anything wrong right now."
Jimmy: "No he can't. He's playing aggressive and he's
playing to win. One more rack and he will be mentioned
among some of the best players in the game today."

Joe breaks rack 18, looks over the table, a routine out for
any player. Joe tightens up a bit and plays positioning a
little more cautiously, no thoughts in his mind other than the
shot. He gets down to the 9 ball but under strokes the leave.
He goes for the difficult cut shot and leaves the 9 ball
hanging in the pocket...6-12 Joe. Shane looks to Joe.

133

Shane: "Nice shooting, but it's my turn now."

Shane gets his break working and makes it 12-12 with little complication. Before Shane breaks the final rack he walks over to Joe and shakes his hand.

Shane: "Great match, you shoot a hell of a game, good luck."
Joe: "It's been a real pleasure, no matter what happens this has been a lot of fun."

Shane breaks the final rack and makes the 2 ball. It's a favorable layout that, if he can get to it, leaves a 6 to 9 combo. The 1 ball in the side is an easy pot, the three ball drops in the corner but Shane uses the whole pocket to get it in. His positioning on the 4 ball isn't ideal but he makes it and gets a shot on the 5 ball. He shoots the 5 ball with a ton of follow but jaws it, the cue ball hits it again and puts the 5 ball in, the cue ball comes off the end rail and floats to mid-table leaving the 6 to 9 combo. It is not a dead on combination. Shane measures the shot out very carefully and approaches it...he misses it. The 9 ball hit both nipples and came up on the long rail about a quarter diamond. Shane got a fortunate roll though. All 4 remaining object balls are against the rail and the cue ball is right behind them. The 9 ball is a quarter diamond from the pocket, the 6 ball is another quarter diamond away from the 9, the 7 and 8 are a half diamond higher up the rail and the cue ball almost

134

touching the 8.

Chris: "Wow, can you feel the tension in this room, what a tough shot that was."
Jimmy: "Combination shots are not gimmie shots Chris, they don't leave any room for error."
Chris: "So what are Joe's options here?"
Jimmy: "Joe's going to need some luck here Chris, he can't just get a hit or play safe. Any miss and he loses, he must make a ball. He does have some options but none of them are great. He might choose to kick/bank the 6 ball but that doesn't leave him anything on the 7 ball. He might be able to 2-rail kick the 6 but I'm not sure the cue ball will pass the 7 ball. I really don't know what he's going to do here. At hill hill for $25,000.00 I wouldn't want this shot. There's nothing he can leave here where Shane wouldn't get out."

Joe looks the table over intently, looking over every possible angle. He then asks the referee if he can take his 10-minute match break now. The referee asks the tournament director and they decide to allow it. Instead of using it as a bathroom break Joe just returns to his chair and ponders the shot, knowing it's all on the line right here. The time goes by quickly and the referee announces the 9 minute mark. Joe gets up and sits by Shane.

Joe: "You've had a hell of a career and you are one of the best ambassadors the game has ever had. Many players look

up to you."
Shane shaking his hand: "Thank you."
Joe: "How many times have you won this event?"
Shane: "5 times."
Joe smiling: "Well my friend, 6 is gonna have to wait, it's my turn."
Shane: "Go get it Joe, you've earned it so far."
Joe: "Thank you."

Joe walks back to his chair and grabs his new cue and again looks at the engraving. He approaches the table and looks at the gap between the 8 ball and the cue ball and gets in a massé stance.

Jimmy: "Well, looks like he's going to massé this shot...I like it, go for the win kid!"

Joe takes a couple practice strokes and repositions himself. Most of the audience and pro's who stuck around to watch is on their feet trying to get a better view. It's so quiet you could hear a mouse fart on the other side of the room. His cue stick straight up and down, Joe strikes down hard on the cue ball. As if in slow motion, the cue ball curves around the 8 and 7 and strikes the far side of the 6 ball. It caroms of the 6 bumps the rail and hits the 9 ball. The 9 ball slowly moves towards the pocket, everyone wondering if it has the speed. The 9 ball slowly rolls past the nipple to the edge of the pocket...and barely falls in. The crowd erupts, everyone

on their feet. Joe lays his stick on the table and begins
weeping. Shane walks over to Joe and hugs him pulling
Joe's head to his shoulder.

Shane: "Hell of a shot, that was the shot of the tournament."
Joe crying: "Thank you sir, I can't believe it."

Shane holds Joe's hand up in victory then steps slightly aside
and joins in the clapping from everyone else. Joe looks out
into the crowd and sees his father with his head in his hands,
Elijah to his left clapping as hard as he can, the rest of the
crowd giving him a standing ovation. Pops comes out of the
crowd.

Pops overtaken with emotion hugging his son: "I'm so
proud of you, I don't even know what else to say."
Joe trying to wipe his face: "That's all I wanted to hear you
say. Thank you Dad."

<u>The Beginning</u>:

With Pops headed back to Chicago Joe takes the next 5 days to take in much of what Vegas has to offer, sights, gambling and girls. Exhausted from the previous 2 weeks activities he's anxious to return to T.J.'s and celebrate with his teacher.

Arriving back in Jackson he finds the pool hall parking lot packed. Walking in he sees just every table being used but it's strangely quiet, no laughter, no music, not even much chatter, just the sound of the balls and the occasional squeak from a chalked cue stick.

Marissa leaning over the counter; "Hey Joe, Lisa's in the backroom waiting for you."
Joe: "The backroom? I can go back there?"
Marissa: "Yup, today you can."
Joe: "Wow, Priest back there too?"

Marissa doesn't answer, just walks back to the kitchen area. Joe walks to the rear of the pool hall and opens the door to the back room. He sees Lisa and Kandy sitting next to each other holding hands on a very large sectional sofa, something that looks like it was custom made. The girls are not dressed in their usual sexy outfits. In the center of the room is a covered table, to the left and the right are several Brunswick spectator chairs and areas that seem to be player assigned. The walls are adorned with billiard antiques and

138

photo's of the Priest with various professional players.

Joe: "Is that a Gold Crown?"
Lisa: "Pull the cover off and look."

Joe pulls the cover off and sees the most beautiful table he could imagine. A Gold Crown in black with tournament blue cloth. The word "Priest" is embroidered on top of the head rail in the cloth. Instead of having diamonds there are large silver crosses with real diamonds in the center of them.

Joe: "Jesus."
Lisa running her hand over the table: "The 16 silver crosses are half inch thick solid silver, the two in the middle of the short rails are solid gold and the same thickness. Those are full 2 carat African diamonds in the middle of every cross. The corner moldings are solid silver, the feet are plated. "Priest" was embroidered with Egyptian silk thread. The pocket liners are custom made water buffalo, the ball return is lined with imported Japanese soft leather. Before assembly each rail was measured every half inch for hardness and rebound consistency. Part of the support frame is made from petrified wood found by a friend from Russia, it dates back to over 4 million years old. All of the bolts and retainers were custom made by ARP and have the same strength as the ones they use in supercharged race engines. The name Brunswick on the side is not painted or a sticker, the name was actually hand embossed into the wood then

filled with ground and powdered shark teeth, then cleared over. The 3" slate took 3 months to make, it's one piece straight from Italy, completely polished with a mirror smooth finish and a .0005 thickness tolerance from one end to the other, no table in the world plays more true. To accommodate the extra weight there's an additional foot on this table, directly in the middle, it happens to be hand carved from marble extracted from an ancient Roman coliseum."

Joe: "My God, what an incredible piece of art, what's something like this cost?"

Lisa: "It's not something you'll see in the Brunswick catalog, it took them 2 years to make working nearly around the clock. We paid 2 million, we've had offers on it up to 7 million but it's never been for sale."

Joe: "Wow, this is just amazing."

Lisa: "This table holds a lot of stories Joe and just about any Pro you can name has come to play on it with the Priest."

Joe: "Yeah, where is he?"

Lisa taking a deep breath: "He passed away last Sunday."

Joe: "Excuse me?"

Lisa: "Have a seat."

Joe sits on the couch and Lisa retains her position next to Kandy. Joe is visibly becoming upset as his eyes begin welling up.

Joe: "What happened?"

Lisa: "Nothing that wasn't expected Joe."

Joe: "What do you mean?"

Lisa: "About a week before your father contacted him he was diagnosed with cancer and a heart condition. At the time he was given 6 months to live. Treatment may have only extended it 2 or 3 months so he declined it."

Joe tears rolling down his face, he stands.

Joe: "Oh my God, why?"

Lisa: "Why what Joe?"

Joe: "Why not take the treatment, 2 months is better than no months."

Lisa: "What kind of 2 months would it have been Joe? Being constantly tired from chemo? Totally out of it because of medications? Hospice? He went out how he lived his life, his way, and I respect him for that."

Joe: "This isn't happening, it's not fair, he didn't even get to see me win."

Lisa: "Well...actually he did."

Joe still crying: "Tell me everything."

Lisa: "Are you sure?"

Joe: "Yes...please."

Lisa: "A couple days after you left he was having bad chest pains, he knew it was close, that's when I called your dad and ordered his ticket. The day before the tournament started he had a massive stroke. At the hospital the Doctors

141

gave him only a couple hours, he turned that into 3 days all on heart. He was coherent and refused the pain medication so he could watch your tournament. He was paralyzed completely on the left side, Kandy and I held devices for him the whole time so he could watch the tournament. He was trying so hard to give you instructions and cheer as you played. The pain had to be unbearable, tears were constantly on his face. I asked him to take something, he refused. When you beat Shane, when that final ball fell, he looked at us and smiled and said "I knew he'd do it, now I can go." We kissed him and both of us held his hands, he passed about 10 minutes later, smiling."

Kandy: "We both lost it, doctors had to give us Valium to calm us down."

Joe crying uncontrollably: "This can't be it..."

Lisa: "It's not Joe, not by a long shot. The three of us did a lot of talking and planning in that final week, T.J.'s will still go on, Kandy and I will still go on, you will still go on..."

Joe: "Right, just he doesn't go on..."

Lisa: "Well...that's not entirely true either Joe."

Joe: "What do you mean?"

Lisa: "Throughout our time together I gave him a lot of things from women to sticks, the one thing I really wanted to give him I couldn't. When I met Kandy I thought she was the perfect one to do it for me and as we grew on her she agreed, she wanted to do it. She's been carrying his child for about 2 months now."

Joe: "No way, did he know?"

Kandy: "Oh Yeah, as soon as I find out I told them both."

Joe: "How's that going to work?"

Lisa: "We're both going to be "mom", we are going to get married, we talked about it a few months ago."

Joe: "Wow, I don't know what to say, this is all so sad and yet so amazing, I can't stop crying."

Kandy: "Us either, we're fine for a minute then it starts all over again, that's why we're back here."

Joe: "A lot is going to change isn't it?"

Lisa: "Yeah, some things will change, the outfits for example may have to change a bit, that was kind of our thing with him, it wouldn't be very special anymore."

Joe: "The pool hall?"

Lisa: "The pool hall has to stay, we're raising a mini Priest."

Joe: "You know it's a boy?"

Kandy rubbing her stomach: "Oh yes."

Lisa: "Asides from maybe the outfits Joe not a whole lot will change, we still have a business to run, pool will still go on, we still have bills to pay and a life to lead, and her and I have a child to raise. In addition to all of that we still want to promote what the Priest was all about and help those who desire it. His words has helped many people through the years,that doesn't have to stop."

Joe: "I'd like to help but don't know what I can do."

Lisa: "Well Joe, we talked about that too, you have a job here for as long as you want it."

Joe: "I can't be a dishwasher or janitor my whole life."

Lisa: "That's not exactly what I meant. It turns out the

house Pro position has opened up...and it comes with a full sponsorship package."

Joe: "Are you kidding me? You'd have me on as a house Pro?"

Lisa: "I wouldn't, I suggested the Sandman, but the Priest would. I don't know that you're ready but he asked me to offer it to you."

Joe: "What would I have to do?"

Lisa: "Well, you'll help out around here as you have been, run some weekend tournaments, give lessons, help spread the messages the Priest was teaching, learn how to replace tips and stuff because Dave won't be around forever either. You'll get a full salary and we'll cover costs to any 6 major tournaments a year. Also, Priest talked to the Sandman a couple months ago, he's on standby for anything we need."

Joe: "I don't think anyone in their right mind would turn that down. Do I get to play on this table?"

Lisa smiling: "Don't push the perks Joe. There is one other catch, and it's not negotiable."

Joe: "What's that?"

Lisa: "You have to either finish high school or get your GED."

Joe: "I can do that and I will do that."

Lisa: "Good to hear it."

Joe: "You said this table has a lot of stories, what's your favorite?'

Kandy: "Probably when he first took her on it, she's told me that one a few times."

144

Joe smiling: "I don't think I'm in the mood to hear that one just quite yet."

Kandy: "The way she tells it, I get soaked every time just listening to her."

Lisa: "That is definitely one of my favorites, seems like we have that on video too, I'll have to look. But I think a more interesting story for Joe might be when Earl lectured me on sharking because I crossed my legs."

Joe: "Earl Strickland?"

Lisa: "Yeah. He was shooting down this way towards where I was sitting on the couch. I had on my usual mini-skirt, I wasn't wearing panties that day. He got down to shoot and I didn't think anything about it I just happened to cross my legs when he was down on the shot. I seriously wasn't trying to go all Basic Instinct on him and distract him I was just changing positions, he got a little upset saying "Most people would consider that sharking lady, a lot of guys would be throwing you out of the room for a move like that." I told him I didn't mean it and he said he knew I didn't but wanted me to understand that most players would have been pissed, but shit the way he was acting I was pretty sure he was pissed."

Joe: "Earl wouldn't be Earl if he wasn't chirping about something. Who won that match?"

Lisa: "Earl. They played a few times Earl always played him tough, Priest only beat him once if I remember right. Earl loved playing on this table."

Joe: "It was quiet when I came in, do all of those people out

145

there know?"

Lisa: "He certainly knew a lot of people, yes, they all know and came in to support the business, it's been packed all week."

Joe: "When was the funeral?"

Lisa: "Couple days ago."

Joe: "That was quick."

Lisa: "After he was diagnosed we had made all the necessary arrangements, including the headstone, all they had to do was the date, they put the headstone down yesterday. Did you want to go see him?"

Joe: "Could I...please?"

Lisa, Kandy and Joe drive out to the cemetery on the other side of town. It's a quiet country setting off the main road. As they park Kandy squeezes Lisa's hand hard and starts crying...

Lisa cupping Kandy's face with her hand then hugs her: "It'll be ok, I promise."

Kandy: "This will never get easier."

Lisa: "Not for awhile, I know, we'll get through it together, we have to."

Lisa and Kandy lead Joe to the grave.

Joe: "Now that is fitting, a huge headstone shaped like a temple, 8 balls on the sides, crossed sticks on the front, that is really cool."

Lisa: "Yup, the three of us designed it together, the temple was Kandy's idea."

Kandy: "It was very hard to not say anything to anyone but that's how he wanted it, he didn't want people pitying him, think Mr.Burnett was the only one who knew anything, and that was "just in case"."

Joe: "Lot of flowers around, who left the sticks?"

Lisa: "I'm not sure, I think they're just symbolic, they're not expensive cues."

Kandy whispering into Lisa's ear: "You wearing panties?"

Lisa whispering back: "Yeah."

Kandy: "I want us to do something for him that he would appreciate and laugh about. Joe, turn around for a minute please."

Lisa: "Oh yeah, I know where you're headed with this, he'd love it, turn around Joe."

Joe complies as the girls remove their jeans and panties. They put their jeans back on and drape their lace panties on the top on the headstone.

Lisa: "Ok Joe."

Joe turns around, then smiles: "Damn, you made me miss the gratuitous butt shot, but yeah, that's him, now he has everything."

Joe tearing up again: "My God he was good wasn't he?"

Lisa smiling putting a finger on her lips looking all flirty:

147

"Oh yeah...and he sure could play some pool too."
Joe laughing: "I wouldn't know about all that other stuff."
Kandy: "Take our word for it, he was a game changer, he should have wrote a book on pleasure, maybe you should."
Lisa: "Maybe I will, we certainly have the experience for it."
Joe: "You're not going to try to replace him are you?"
Lisa: "Oh fuck no, there's no replacing him. We don't need anther man in our life but if we wanted to "play" I'd call the Sandman, he's accustomed to this type of relationship. He already has a commitment and the only man I'd trust to keep things at a level I want them at, and his girls trust me, so, that would be it. But there will never be another guy in our relationship."
Joe: "It's funny, I tried to channel him at the tournament, especially on that final shot."
Lisa smiling: "You probably did Joe. When you took the break and sat down just to think the shot over he was lying in the bed and kept saying 4:30, 4:30 over and over again like he was trying to channel you, and when you made it we all got goosebumps. You put on a hell of a performance and he saw all of it."
Joe crying: "And 4:30 is where I hit it, I just felt it, I felt him tell me. Could I have a minute with him?"
Lisa: "Absolutely, and you can come here anytime as well, he'd like that."

Kandy and Lisa walk back to the car.

Joe kneeling at the grave wiping his face: "In a world of artificial, you were the realist. I can't name anyone who would want to spend the last few months of their life stuck in a pool hall training some no name hack player like myself. Anybody else would be trying to get things off of their to do list before they die or they'd be wallowing around in self pity saying "why me", you were too genuine for that. Lisa told me one time that most of the people you interact with you guys consider acquaintances because people are so fake. And they are, I don't know how many people say one thing to your face and yet something different behind your back, people do suck. I don't know what category you placed me in but with everything you did for me I like to think you thought of me as a real friend. I will spend the rest of my life showing you that you weren't wrong to feel that way about me. They probably don't need it, they're strong willed and minded but I will always be there for Lisa and Kandy and make sure nobody messes with them, they say jump I'll say how high, I know what they meant to you. Your child will never want for anything I'll make sure of that, I won't over step any bounds set by moms' but I'll be a great Uncle for him. And I will do my best to teach him, and anyone else, the game as you've taught it to me. You've left some pretty big shoes to fill and set some pretty high bars for both living life and representing the game. You did these things with such grace and ease, so naturally, it's going to be tough to maintain that level like you did...but I think not impossible. I don't believe in God, but I believe in you,

149

and with all the things you wanted me to understand I hope that is something you can understand."

Back at the pool hall.

Sitting and staring at table 14, remembering the lessons, remembering watching him play, remembering his words, his moves, completely lost in thought of The Priest, a shadow across his face interrupts him, he turns slowly to see Efren Reyes...

Efren speaking softly: "You ready young man?"

Joe looking like a deer in headlights turns to Lisa...

Joe: "What am I supposed to do now?"
Lisa almost shouting: "What do you mean what are you supposed to do now? The Priest gave you the last 6 months of his life, he trained you to be a champion, be that Joe, be a champion, be a fucking legend..."

Joe stands and walks to the backroom door, his head hanging low. Grasping the ornate door handle he pauses and takes a very deep breath, he raises his head then slowly turns to look at Efren.

Joe: "I am Sir."

150

To be continued...

Thank you for reading part 1 of Massé, I hope you found it not typical of a pool story. We have several movies on pool but in essence they are all the same. They're about gambling, hustling, dumping matches, sharking, someone getting hurt because of it, someone getting screwed over...it's always the same thing. I didn't want that for Massé because there's more to pool than what our movies or gossip would have you believe. There are good people in this sport from every race and nationality. There are thousands of inspirational stories that come from pool, these are the stories that should be told. Pool doesn't care about your disability, sexual orientation, race, religion, political view, how fat or how skinny you are, whether you're male or female...this game is played by people from ALL walks of life, from billionaires to people who can't rub two pennies together. Pool is quite unique in this aspect. Pool has another unique aspect though, those who play it represent the whole instead of the one. What that means is simply this, your actions, as a player, is reflected on the whole sport. When people who don't play the game hear stories it's usually a story about a fight, or a bet gone bad, or some player cheating. And the person hearing the story tends to believe these stories encompasses ALL of pool...everybody's a shark, everybody's a gambler, everybody's a cheater...this is not even close to truth, but this is the game's reputation because no one will stand up and say "No, this is not how it should be." Yes, as a hustler I contributed to the sports reputation but I've spent that last several years trying to make amends for that because I learned. Everyone who plays the game wants it to be greater, bigger prizes, more recognition, better sponsors, more players, to be in the Olympics...but the players themselves don't want to change for it. Stories like Massé get swept under the rug in favor of a gambling match. People are entertained more by tragedy than inspiration, this in itself is a tragedy. Watching someone fail shouldn't make yourself feel better, at least they had the guts to try. What does that say about you? There's a major underdog somewhere who just won a local tournament, they had to face a lot of internal battles to win, but you'll never hear that story, you're more likely to hear about some Pro gap racking or playing a $20,000 "action" match. You're more likely to hear amateurs jerking off their ego about tight pockets, table brands, and best tip/cue claims. Pool is really a beautiful game played by ugly people, but truth is, people are just ugly in general. People lie, break speed limits, cheat on their taxes, disregard commitments, throw trash anywhere and everywhere...pool's got nothing to do with being human. The only difference between pool and other "legitimate" sports is that other sports are well organized, have top notch leadership and hold their humans accountable. One variant or another of Pocket billiards is played in every single country on the planet, and it's the oldest surviving sport, it is the "Adam" all of played sports today. But because pool has never been well led or organized it is a direct reflection of society, it's society's game. The stories you hear within it are no different than stories you hear from outside of it. People lie, cheat, gamble and steal everyday to get what they want, and they don't play pool. It's not a pool problem, it's a people problem. It may not help the respect of the sport though if we keep it in bars and casinos. But I think if you're going to play a sport, like pool, you should represent it better, knowing that you represent all of us as well, not just yourself. I would like to think this is a good time to hear some new stories instead of the same old regurgitated ones. I hope you enjoyed Massé. I understand it may not be everyone's cup of tea, but...what is?

Until next time,
Tim

Support your local pool hall!

Made in the USA
Las Vegas, NV
28 May 2021

23805551R00095